A Stone Unturned

A Mystery Novel

Khadijah McDonald Carey

A Stone Unturned is a work of fiction. Names, characters, businesses, events, and incidents are the products of the author's imagination. Any resemblance to actual persons, living or dead, actual events, or locations is purely coincidental.

A Stone Unturned
Copyright © 2019 by Khadijah McDonald Carey

ISBN 978-0-578-55460-0

Cover Design by Krisanna Adamovic, K&A Design, LLC

Dedication

This book is dedicated to my beloved grandmother Alice Carrington whose sudden passing removed the log that was suffocating my fire. I was forced to realize that I cannot waste any more time on this Earth. Now with the log removed, my fire can breathe freely and for that, I thank you and love you dearly. Praise to the Lord always for His endless love and favor, and the gifts He has given me to share with the world. I am nothing without you, Lord. Lastly, thanks to my husband, my four beautiful children, and my parents and siblings for the love and encouragement that you continue to show me.

Chapter 1

Megan peered out of her bedroom window. She cried as she watched her father being carried away by two strange men in black suits. Her mother's screams didn't help the situation and they only confirmed to Megan that something was wrong. Megan had run to her bedroom, not only to see her father for what she believed was the last time but to also get away from her mother's high-pitched hysteria.

Tears streamed down Megan's face as she watched the men push her dad into a black car and drive away.

"Megan!"

A familiar voice caused Megan to snap out of her train of thought.

"I'm sorry, Laney. What were you saying?"

"I was asking if you wanted to have the event at the Gashange's Gallery. It's sure to pull in a big crowd."

"Yeah, sure," Megan said nonchalantly.

"Are you okay? You've been out of it all day it seems. Every time I try to talk to you, you're in space. What's up?"

"Nothing...just got a lot on my mind, that's all."

"Mm, hmm," Laney said not believing one word. "Well I'm gonna go have Tracey draw up the plan for the event, then I'll reach out to Sam over at Gashange's."

"Okay, let me know when everything's done," said Megan.

"Yup, always do." Laney hurried out of Megan's office and closed the door behind her.

Megan sat twiddling her thumbs. She wasn't in the mood for anything today. Especially since she couldn't keep her mind from drifting to everything but work.

Dinner with mom at 6, she thought, *gotta do something to get out of that.*

Ding!

An email alert went off on her computer. It was from Laney.

Megan frowned. "How the heck did she get to her office so fast?" she said aloud. "I swear that girl is like the Energizer Bunny or something."

Normally Megan would be impressed with Laney's overzealous dedication to getting the job done, but not today.

Megan quickly read the email and began typing a response. She typed for a few seconds and then stopped. Frustrated, she leaned back in her chair and stared off into space. She was back at it again, thinking about the past. She couldn't help it though. Today marked the 20th anniversary of when her father was taken from their home. Her family was having breakfast when they were interrupted by the doorbell. Megan's father was just in the middle of telling her the secret to how he made his pancakes so fluffy and moist. Her mother went to answer the door and before anyone knew it, two burly men rushed into the house and headed straight for the kitchen. One man looked to be Italian, and the other was black.

"*Get up and do it slowly,*" Megan remembered the Italian one say to her father. Her father did as the man said. As soon as he stood up, both men immediately grabbed him on each side and pushed him toward the door. Her father didn't fight, he just went along.

Megan never saw her father again after that and she never knew exactly what happened to him. All she was sure of was that the men who took him were big and they had guns. Still, she remembered her father being fearless that day, telling her not to cry and to be a big girl for her mother and little brother. As a ten-year-old girl, she tried to be as brave as she could at that moment. She figured she was brave simply because she didn't scream as her mother did. Instead, she remained calm so she could hear everything her father was saying to her.

She closed her eyes as she allowed the memory of his last words spoken to her play in her mind. "Always prepare yourself, baby girl. Most importantly, always assess the situation." Her father said all he could before he was completely taken out of the house. Yet, Megan never knew exactly what he'd meant by those last words. The mysterious disappearance of her father had caused those words to haunt her in her adult years.

"I can't do this today," Megan told herself as she stood from her desk. She grabbed her pocketbook and headed out the door. As she made her way down the hallway she was spotted by Laney.

"Hey Meg, I was waiting for you to respond to my email."

"Can't right now. Gotta go, something's come up," Megan said dryly.

"What?!... We've been trying to get this event together for weeks. Everything is just now coming together; you can't leave now," Laney said in a panic.

"I said something's come up. I'll see you in the morning," Megan replied authoritatively.

Laney stood helpless and confused as she watched her boss walk out of the office building.

Megan hopped into her car and slammed the door. She was suddenly overwhelmed with emotions both angry and sad. She let out a scream and punched the middle of the steering wheel causing the horn to beep. She quickly wiped the tears that fell from her eyes. She hated this time of year. She was always strong all year round until this day came upon her. Year after year she told herself that she would handle it differently, that she wouldn't let her emotions get in the way of her work, and that she would create positive ways to honor her father's memory. Yet, each year she failed.

Maybe I should go back inside, she thought. It's what she wished she could do but couldn't. So, she started her car and pulled off.

Chapter 2

Megan pulled her car into the West Care Medical Pavilion and found a parking space. She pulled down her car's sun visor and took a hard look in the mirror. *I don't look too bad,* she thought. She patted her eyes dry with a tissue, reapplied some gloss on her lips and closed the sun visor. She grabbed her pocketbook, stepped out of the car and made her way toward the building.

"Welcome to West Care, how may I help you?" the receptionist asked Megan almost as soon as she walked through the door.

"Ah, yes I'm here to see Dr. Franklin please."

"Sure, just sign-in on the clipboard and have a seat while I get you registered."

"I'm sorry, I'm not here for an actual doctor's visit. I just need to see him."

The receptionist looked as if she wasn't sure what to make of Megan's request. Realizing her confusion, Megan further explained.

"It's more of an in and out thing... and he's expecting me. So, if you could just give him a call and let him know I'm here that would be great." Megan flashed a phony smile.

"Okay, sure. I'll let him know," the receptionist said. She nervously smiled back at Megan while dialing Dr. Franklin's extension.

Megan couldn't understand why the girl was so nervous.

Maybe she's new, Megan thought. *I sure have never seen her before.*

"Dr. Franklin, there's a woman here to see you, she says you're expecting her...uh yes, her name is –

The receptionist looked at Megan for the answer.

"Megan...Megan Stone."

"Megan Stone, Sir," repeated the receptionist, "okay will do." She hung up the phone and stepped out from behind the counter, then opened a door that led to a long hallway.

"The doctor will see you in his office, Ms. Stone. You're going to go straight down this hall and it's the last door on your right."

Megan already knew this, still, she smiled politely at the young lady and said: "thank you."

"My pleasure," the receptionist replied and walked back to her desk.

Megan made her way down the hall to Dr. Franklin's office. The door was open, but she gave a gentle knock to let him know she was there.

Dr. Franklin looked up from a file he was reading and smiled at Megan.

"Hey Meg, come in, come in," he said as he stood up from his desk and walked toward her.

"Hey, Liam," Megan whispered. She couldn't hold back any longer and burst into tears.

Liam rushed to console her.

"It's okay, shh, shh," he spoke gently as he pulled her into himself. Megan buried her face in Liam's chest and sobbed quietly. She didn't mean to start crying again, and she most certainly didn't want to be loud about it in Liam's place of business.

"I'm sorry, Liam. This wasn't my intention," she told him as she lifted her head from his chest.

"Meg, it's okay, really. I know this day has always been tough for you."

Megan sighed. "That's why I came to you first. You're the only one who's ever understood what this day does to me. How it's tortured me, and still does."

"You know I got you, girl," Liam said as he wrapped his arms around her.

Megan felt safe for the first time all day. She knew that coming to see Liam would help her get a grip on things. He had a gentle spirit about him that made her feel at ease whenever she was going through something.

"You're always there for me," she told him. "Someone like me needs a friend like you."

"Dido," he said, then kissed her on the forehead and wiped her tears. He gently parted from their embrace and turned around to pull out one of the office chairs so Megan could sit down.

As Megan took her seat, Liam also returned to his desk and sat down.

"Thanks for seeing me. I know you weren't expecting me today." She paused for a moment, then chuckled lightly as she remembered the fib she told at the front desk. "I guess that made your receptionist pretty nervous out there, huh?"

Liam laughed. "Yeah, I guess it did. Especially since she knows my schedule, which doesn't include non-medical visits or pop-ups."

"I hear you, but why is she so nervous though?"

"Well, I guess it's because she's new. Plus, the last receptionist was fired for letting all sorts of stuff happen. She hardly took messages and the biggest problem was that she didn't screen calls."

"Yeah, that would be a problem."

"Yup, so there was a vote and the majority of the physicians wanted her gone, so that's that."

"Well that explains it, doesn't it?" Megan smiled. Her eyes met his and they locked for a moment, then Megan quickly looked away.

Liam cleared his throat. "Meg, you may not have been on my schedule today, but I *was* expecting you. I want you to know that."

"Please don't make me cry again," she said as she hung her head in embarrassment. Hearing Liam say this only confirmed that she could always count on him. Still, she didn't like looking him in the eyes. At least not for long. There was something there in his eyes that she didn't want to ever explore. There were a few occasions where their eyes locked, and she felt her heart melt. It scared her, and she didn't like it. She loved Liam without a doubt, but not as a lover, only a true friend. At least that's what she trained herself to believe. There were times when she wished there could've been more between them. However, the thought of messing up such a good friendship discouraged the notion every time it popped up. Besides, she'd never been in love before and never had much success dating. She dealt with a few frogs here and there, and maybe even one prince; her ex-boyfriend Sean, but Megan was looking for a king.

She could see that Liam would be *that* king for the woman he married. Sometimes, the thought alone made her jealous, and she'd beat herself up about how ridiculous she was to be jealous of a woman whom neither she nor Liam has even met. Still, she knew the day would come because Liam was the perfect catch. He was a handsome, successful young black doctor with smooth brown skin and almond-shaped eyes. He kept his hair cut low, a dark Caesar with waves and a neat mustache and goatee. He was also tall with a firm muscular built, courtesy of the gym four times a week. Yes, he would not be on the market for much longer. Once he got married or even engaged, Megan knew she would have to take a back seat. It made her sad to think about, but it was only right. She wasn't in the business for being the type of woman who stayed friends with a man after he became married. "*The wife and kids come first,*" she heard her father's voice say. He taught her that when she was just five years old, and there was no way she would go against it. She valued every lesson dearly.

"Meg, I need you to listen to me, sweetheart, and don't take this the wrong way." Liam's tone was serious but gentle as always.

Megan looked up at him, slightly nervous about what he was going to say.

"You know you can always talk to me, but I think you should finally seek some professional help."

"You mean like a psychiatrist or something?" Megan was quickly annoyed by the suggestion.

"Yes, but not a psychiatrist. I know you ain't crazy, girl. Sheesh, cut me some slack," Liam said between laughs. His laughter caused Megan to lighten up.

"Okay... then like a therapist?"

Liam nodded.

Megan looked down and picked at her French manicured nails. She thought for a moment, then sighed deeply.

"Okay, fine. I'll do it."

"For real?!" Liam was surprised but relieved. He wasn't sure how the conversation would go and the last thing he wanted to do was hurt or upset her.

"Yes, for real. So, I'm guessing you have a referral for me since this is your genius plan," she said with a hint of sarcasm.

"Come on, don't be like that. But yes, I do have a referral for you," Liam said as he reached for a card on his desk. "This lady right here is the best. She works wonders for my patients." He handed Megan the card.

"I see you were prepared. Been thinking 'bout this much?" she asked as she slid the card into her pocketbook.

Liam could see that Megan was becoming defensive.

"It's not like that, sweetheart. I told you, I was expecting you."

Megan shifted and crossed her arms. She knew Liam was telling the truth. However, she couldn't help being overly sensitive.

"I'm sorry, Liam. It's not you. You of all people know that on this day everything rubs me the wrong way."

"I know."

"I know you're just trying to help, and I appreciate it."

"Will you give her a call?" he asked with pleading eyes.

"Yes, I will," Megan said reassuringly. "I promise."

Liam smiled. "Wanna have dinner tonight at my place? I'll call up my chef and order a masseuse just for you."

Megan stood to her feet. "I'd absolutely love that, but I have reservations tonight with my mom at six."

"Ouch," Liam said, knowing she wasn't looking forward to that.

"Yeah, tell me about it. I get to sit and listen to her complain about rich people's problems."

"Hey, don't front. You're a part of those rich folk too now," he teased. "Miss front page cover."

"I was not on the front page, Liam, stop it."

"Might as well have been. What was it, the second or third page?"

Megan playfully scowled at Liam. "The point is, I've worked hard to maintain my wealth, Liam, and you have too. Meanwhile, my mom has stayed rich by keeping a rich man."

"I hear ya," Liam said not wanting to touch that subject. "Anyway, come give me some love, woman. I gotta get ready for my next patient."

Megan walked over to Liam and they hugged each other tightly.

"Thanks again, Liam. I needed this."

"Anything for you, Meg," he said as he kissed her forehead.

Megan grabbed her pocketbook off the chair and walked toward the door.

"Oh, and I want a raincheck for dinner at your place," she said turning around. "That private chef and masseuse sound too good to pass up."

"You got it. Just let me know."

"No. You call me, and I'll make time...like you always do for me."

"Even better," he smiled warmly.

Megan suddenly felt her heart flutter. *There it goes,* she thought. *I hate when that happens.* Still, she smiled back at him and walked out the door.

17

As she left the office, Megan decided that she would stop by the San Diego River to clear her head. She needed some time alone in a peaceful environment before having dinner with her mother.

Chapter 3

Megan pulled up in front of Helena's, her mother's favorite restaurant. She unlocked her door as the valet approached her car. He opened her door and held it as she stepped out.

"Madame," he politely greeted her.

"Hello Sir," Megan said as she gently placed her car keys in his hand. "Take good care of my baby," Megan told him in reference to her white on white Mercedes-Maybach S650 Cabriolet.

"Of course, madame."

Megan started up the stairs to the restaurant. As she entered, she took a deep breath hoping to relieve her anxiety and better prepare herself for dinner with her mother, Keres. She wanted to be able to talk to Keres about how her day was going and how she felt about her dad's disappearance. However, every year it was the same old thing with her mother, and she never wanted to talk about it.

Hopefully, today will be different, Megan thought.

"Ms. Stone, how are you?" A young hostess said as Megan walked up to the host station.

"I'm doing well, Diana," Megan lied.

"Awesome. You can find Mrs. Danes in the usual booth. Would you like me to escort you?"

"No, I'll be fine. Thanks."

"Okay, enjoy."

"Thank you," Megan said. She made her way to the back of the restaurant where she spotted her mother sitting in her favorite booth.

"Sweetheart," her mother said as Megan approached the table.

Keres got up to kiss her daughter on the cheek.

"Hey mom," Megan said as she gave her mother a tight squeeze.

"You're almost late, honey. I'm hungry and ready to order. Sit down."

"I'm sorry. I stopped by the river...you know, the part where dad used to take me fishing."

"Mm-hmm," Keres said as if to say, *'please don't start,'* but she didn't want to hurt Megan's feelings.

"Yeah, I stopped over there just to clear my head a little."

Keres grinned slightly. Megan could see through her mother's fake smile and courtesy that she was already growing impatient.

"Well, I hope you were successful. Especially since I was hoping we could talk about less depressing matters," said Keres sternly.

Megan lowered her eyes. Although she expected her mother's response, she couldn't help feeling disappointed.

Keres quickly noticed Megan's dissatisfaction and reached across the table to gently take hold of her hand.

"Meg, why can't we just sit and enjoy each other's company without dwelling on the past?"

Megan shrugged. She needed time before she could speak again. If she spoke now, she would just burst into tears. She hated that she always had to appear strong in front of her mother. Yet, it was no fault of her own. Keres was a bit of a hard woman who hadn't displayed a sad emotion in years. Unfortunately, she didn't allow her kids to express their emotions either.

While the abduction of her husband was a traumatizing experience for Megan, it was mind-numbing for Keres. So much so, she wouldn't allow anyone to ever talk about it. Whenever anyone brought it up, especially Megan, Keres' response was often cold or dismissive.

Keres' attitude toward the anniversary of her late husband's abduction was the main reason why Megan dreaded having dinner with her this evening. Megan needed to be with someone who would listen to her and not stifle her emotions. Still, here she was, with mommy dearest having to pretend as usual. She was sick of it, but she was going to suck it up.

"I'm sure you've noticed me in *Sky 2020*," Megan said, appeasing her mother by changing the subject.

"I have, and I'm so proud of you," Keres said smiling, then pulling the magazine from her large pocketbook.

"Oh, my goodness, you brought it with you?" Megan said pleasantly surprised.

"Of course I did. What do you think this is? My baby is on the cover of a magazine and I'm not gonna brag?"

Megan blushed. She felt her spirit lifted for the first time since being in her mother's presence.

"It wasn't the cover, mom," Megan said chuckling lightly. "I don't know why people keep saying that."

"Well, it might as well be. Look at this," Keres said opening the magazine to page three and four. "Bam! It's right in your face. All you have to do is open the magazine and there you are. That's cover material, baby girl. I don't care what anyone else says."

"Oh mom," Megan said shyly. "Cut it out, will you?"

"Modest Meg. Always so modest," Keres said shaking her head. "Sometimes I don't know how you became so successful with your timid ways, child. This is something to shout to the hills about."

Megan gave her mother a short nod and pulled the magazine toward her. She looked on in admiration, but it wasn't her style to brag. She'd leave that part to her mother who enjoyed it way more than she did. Besides, if Keres had to brag about something, Megan would rather it be her *Sky 2020* article.

Sky 2020 was no small thing. It was one of the most popular and prestigious business magazines in the country. So, Megan was humbled by the experience especially after working so hard to put her company's name on the map. When she got the call that they wanted to do a featured article on her company, Stone Art Enterprises, she knew her dreams were finally coming true.

Her photo in the magazine looked stunning as well. She had a two-page spread in which she graced the left side of the article in a stylish all-white pantsuit that had visible specks of yellow paint throughout. Her hair was pulled up into a flawless bun and her face hardly touched with just a hint of gold eyeshadow and nude lips. In her left hand, she held a paintbrush that dripped yellow paint onto the floor. On her feet, she wore shiny red stilettos in which the left one displayed a few yellow splashes of paint. It was a beautiful mess of a picture meant to embody the essence of her artistry.

The right side of the spread captured a picture of various artwork in Megan's showroom. The best part of it all was that Stone Art Enterprises was now considered one of the top *Sky 2020* businesses in the country. This took place just two weeks after the issue was published. Megan was ecstatic by the new business she was getting from various parts of the country. It was one of the reasons the event at Gashange's Gallery was so important. It was basically a huge networking event for her new clients.

"You should've been a model, sweetheart," Keres said sliding the magazine back in front of her. "You just look so beautiful."

"Thanks, mom."

"You're welcome." Keres paused momentarily. "It just amazes me how much you look like your father."

Megan looked shockingly at her mother. *There's no way she's talking about my dad right now,* she thought.

"I haven't heard you say I looked like daddy since I was a kid...since before he-"

Keres cleared her throat. "Yeah just the eyes, I guess. I can see him in your eyes."

Megan could see her mother was becoming very uncomfortable. Still, she figured now was her only chance, so she dove in.

"Mom, we have to talk about him at some point. I mean why should we-

"Megan, please...okay? Just stop," Keres interjected. "I should've never brought him up. I'm sorry."

"Well, I'm not. We've been doing this dance for twenty years. When is it going to end?"

"Megan," Keres warned.

"No, come on, mom. This isn't right. You're the only person that experienced it with me, who knows what that nightmare was like, and what it's done to our family and-

"Megan, I said stop!" Keres yelled almost causing a scene.

In a few short moments, a waitress came over to their table.

"I apologize for the wait," said the waitress. "Can I get you some water, or maybe some wine?"

"Yes, lots of wine," said Keres. "We'll take the house vintage."

The waitress then turned to ask Megan what she wanted but Keres shooed her off just as fast.

There was an awkward silence at the table and Megan was visibly upset. Some might even say livid, yet she maintained her composure.

Keres decided not to engage. She wanted to drop the conversation altogether, so she picked up her cell phone and started going through her emails.

Megan leaned back in her seat and crossed her arms. She watched her mother for a few seconds and waited to see if she would look up at her. Megan was too frustrated to have patience and decided to speak her truth. Whether her mother made eye contact, she still had to listen. This time Megan was determined to be heard.

"Mom, I am not going to allow you to do this to me anymore, okay? I need answers and I need to be able to talk about this..."

Keres continued to scroll through her emails.

"For my sanity, and... for healing." Megan's eyes began to well with tears.

Keres finally looked up from her phone. She sighed. "This is how I deal, Meg."

Megan grabbed a napkin from the table and quickly began wiping her tears before the waitress returned.

"How can you cope like that? By never talking about it?"

"It works for me. Maybe not for you, or your brother, but for me, okay? So, I'm gonna say this for the last time, Meg, then I'm gonna need you to leave it at that. Please respect *my* way of coping."

Megan felt defeated. What could she possibly say after that? She had to respect her mother's wishes even if they didn't benefit her.

"Fine, mom," Megan said giving in.

"Thank you," Keres said, a bit relieved.

"But, since I can't talk to you, I think you should know that you've helped me make my decision in seeing a therapist."

"Oh...okay," Keres said. She was slightly caught off guard and wasn't sure how to react. Still, she knew that she couldn't protest after just asking Megan to respect her way of coping.

"I know you haven't been a fan of therapy or psychiatry, but I need to heal. It's time."

"Okay, I can respect that."

There was an awkward pause again.

Megan cleared her throat. "There's one more thing," she said a bit nervous.

"What's that?" Keres asked with a raised brow.

"After I begin therapy and I'm strong enough, I..." Megan paused.

"What, Megan?" Keres probed.

"I-I wanna hire an investigator to help me find out what happened to my dad."

"What?!" Keres was stunned. "Why in the world would you wanna do that, Meg?"

"I need answers, mom...and you won't give me any so-

"I don't have any answers for you, Meg," Keres said assuredly. "The only thing I can tell you is that this is a bad idea."

"Why? Why is it bad?"

"Because your father was into some dangerous things, Meg. I've always told you at least that much."

"Well...I," Megan sighed. She didn't know what else to say. All she knew was that she'd made up her mind. Therapy and then a private investigator.

"Please, baby, don't do this. You could get yourself hurt," Keres pleaded.

"I'll be okay, mom. It's just time I'd get some closure. That's all."

"You can get closure in therapy, Meg."

"Mom, please. I need this. I'm thirty now...I need to move on with my life. I gotta close this chapter."

Keres thought for a moment. She knew her daughter was right.

"Fine, but please be careful," she said worriedly.

"I will, mom."

Chapter 4

It was a beautiful day and the Southern California air was crisp and perfect for Megan's morning jog. She was on her last mile and slowed her pace as she neared her driveway. She stopped by her mailbox to check it. There was nothing in it but a circular. The cool breeze softly brushed against her golden-brown skin and flowed through her long silky black ponytail. She took a moment to bask in the glory of the day by closing her eyes and inhaling and exhaling deeply. She did this a few more times before she proceeded up her driveway.

She felt much lighter today and was ready to take on the world. Everything she neglected to do the day before, she would handle today. As she opened the front door to her house, she realized that she hadn't locked it. She immediately felt uneasy. *Oh gosh,* she thought, *what was I thinking?* She stepped into the house, then turned around to lock the door. Forgetting to lock the door wasn't the end of the world, especially since she had a huge guard dog freely roaming about the house. However, the fact that she forgot to do something that came so natural to her was what bothered her the most. It just further proved to Megan that she made the right choice to finally see a therapist. She didn't want her mind to be so preoccupied with thoughts of the past that she couldn't carry out simple tasks. As for her house, at least she knew Cooper was holding it down for her.

"Cooper, where are you boy?" she called out as she took her running shoes off and left them by the door.

"Coop?" She made her way out of the foyer and into the great room, but there was no sign of him. Suddenly she heard a thump from up above. Megan groaned. She knew where the sound was coming from, so she headed up to her room.

"Please don't be in my shoes, please don't be in my shoes," she chanted prayerfully as she jogged up the steps. She finally got to her bedroom and oddly enough the door was closed. When she opened it, there was Cooper, her 130-pound rottweiler, with one of her manila folders in his mouth. Megan looked around at her room and there were papers all over the floor, some of them were badly chewed up.

"Cooper put that down!" she shouted as she grabbed the folder from his mouth. She then took the same folder and whacked him twice on the nose. "That's a bad boy, Cooper," she said. "You stay out of my room. Go!" she shouted. Cooper hung his head and exited her room.

"You've got to be kidding me," she said aloud. "Then he had the nerve to close himself in here...unbelievable." Megan was beyond irritated. She was having such a good morning until she got back into the house.

She took a few deep breaths to calm herself. "It's okay. We're not gonna let this little mishap kill the positive vibes," she said attempting at self-encouragement. She braced herself as she went to collect the chewed-up documents off the floor. She was afraid to see which documents Cooper had destroyed. She hoped it was just a few drafts of work already completed.

After picking up each document she was happy to see that they were all drafts, just as she hoped. So, she grabbed a medium-sized plastic bag and threw the papers in, to shred later. Afterward, she got undressed and hopped in the shower.

Megan was all dressed and ready to start her day at the office. She had on a canary yellow sundress that was sophisticated enough for the office and grown and sexy enough for cocktails after work. Yet, today was all business for Megan as she had to make up for walking out on Laney yesterday.

Megan stepped into her large walk-in closet and scanned her collection of shoes. She grabbed a pair of comfortable but very cute red pumps. She was about to be on her way when she spotted a crinkled-up picture on the floor. She squinted and bent down to pick it up. It was a small family portrait of her mother, father, brother and herself.

"Ugh, Cooper," she said with a hint of frustration. She examined the crinkled-up picture and noticed that he didn't get a chance to puncture or rip it up with his teeth. Megan let out a sigh of relief. *Thank God*, she thought. She stared at the picture for a moment. She looked at her father's face. How she missed seeing his handsome face. She hadn't looked at this picture in years, and purposefully so. She wondered why now of all days Cooper had to miraculously find it.

As she continued to stare at her father's face in the picture, she suddenly recalled her mother's voice from the night before. *"It just amazes me how much you look like your father."*

Although Megan was honored by her mother's comment, she didn't think she looked that much like her dad. Megan certainly saw that she had his dark brown eyes and his beautiful soft black curly hair. Still, she wasn't the spitting image of him. Megan believed she had her own look for the most part. She figured her parents' genes put up a pretty good fight when it came to her, as she was a couple of shades lighter than her father and a few shades darker than her mother.

As she held the picture in her hand, her eyes landed on her brother, Kent, who was about four years old at the time the picture was taken. Now *he* was the spitting image of Keres, with the same high yellow complexion and captivating blue eyes. The only thing Kent inherited from their father was his curly black hair. Then again, that was hard to get away from being that their father was half black and Sri Lankan.

As Megan stared at the picture, she didn't really know how to feel about it. Anyhow, she was relieved that she didn't feel as bad as she thought she would. She kissed the picture, ensuring that her father's face was the target, then stored it away up high where

Cooper could no longer get to it. She was now ready for work and determined to have a good day.

Megan strolled into the office, coffee in hand and ready to face Laney. Although Megan was Laney's employer, she knew that she had to apologize for walking out on her yesterday. It was bad on her part, especially since she took pride in leading by example. As Megan passed by Laney's office, she poked her head in to let Laney know she'd arrived.

"Good morning," Megan said.

"Good morning, boss lady," Laney responded halfway looking up from her computer.

"I need you to come to my office ASAP."

Megan's request got Laney's full attention and she was now looking directly at Megan.

"Uh, sure. Everything okay?" Laney asked concerned.

"Yes, girl. Just come see me please," Megan said in a playful tone, then walked away toward her office.

Laney immediately felt at ease once she saw that Megan seemed to be in a good mood. She gathered her pen and notepad, locked her computer and walked down the hall to see what Megan wanted.

"You doing okay today, boss?" Laney asked as she entered Megan's office. She always referred to Megan as "boss lady" or "boss" when she wasn't sure which side of Megan she was getting; the friend or the employer. For Laney, it was always best to stay professional whenever there was a question of the matter. She knew not to let personal affairs get in the way of business, which is why Megan kept her around.

"I'm doing much better today. Thanks for asking," Megan replied. "And you can stop with the *boss* talk, alright."

"Phew," Laney said while pretending to wipe sweat off her forehead.

Both the women laughed, and Laney took a seat.

"I'm glad you're feeling better, Meg. We've made lots of progress with our upcoming event. We finally got the-

Megan raised her hand to signal Laney to stop talking. "Before you get into work stuff, I just wanted to apologize for yesterday. I know how hard you work around here to get things done for me, and I shouldn't have left you...not during crunch time anyway."

"You don't have to apologize, Meg. You're a hard worker too. And I'm sure there had to be a good reason for leaving yesterday. I could tell that your mind just wasn't here."

36

"Well, there was a reason but I'm not sure how valid it was for business. But I'd like to explain it to you one day. I think it's time you knew," Megan said matter- of- factly.

"Whenever you're ready, I'm here," Laney replied. She was sincere but more than that, she was curious. Although Megan and Laney's relationship started as boss and employee, they developed a friendship over time. They were close, but not close enough for Megan to tell Laney about the disappearance of her father. Whenever Laney tried to get Megan to open up about her family life, Megan would always divert the conversation back to work. Eventually, Megan finally pulled the *boss* card and told Laney that she thought it was best if they didn't discuss each other's families. Although Laney pretended to understand, she thought the idea was stupid. Especially after both women had already dished out issues regarding past boyfriends and other personal drama. Still, all Laney could do was respect Megan's wishes no matter how lame they seemed.

"So, what were you saying about the event?" Megan asked ready to get back down to business.

"Oh right, we are ready to go with Gashange's. The date is all set, and we have a few new artists that we scouted last week who want to present some fresh work at the auction."

"Great! Let's get to it then. Call an emergency meeting in an hour so we can discuss this with the rest of the team."

"Will do...*boss lady,*" Laney teased.

Megan chuckled and fanned Laney off. As Laney got up and exited the office, Megan grabbed her cell phone to text Liam.

Top of the morning to ya, buddy. Just wanted you to know that I'm feeling much better today and can't wait to have that dinner you promised me ;)...lol

Megan placed her cell phone on her desk and logged on to her computer to check her emails. She had a few requests for hosting art exhibits at various locations and within other art galleries. Megan was happy to see her magazine spread paying off. She took her time responding to each email and checking her calendar for available dates. Afterward, she checked her phone messages and returned a few calls.

Bzzz Bzzz.

Megan's cell phone vibrated. She picked it up and saw that it was Liam returning her text. She was so engaged in her work that she forgot she even texted him.

So glad you're doing better, sweetie. Come by tonight for dinner if you're serious.

Megan smiled. She loved how available Liam made himself for her. She replied to his text:

Is the masseuse gonna be there too? Lol

Bzzz Bzzz.

Megan read Liam's reply: Someone's being demanding, lol.

Megan chuckled.

She replied: Hey, it was your idea.

Bzzz Bzzz

Lol, true. You know I'm just playing, girl. If you want a masseuse, you got it.

"Aww, he's just too sweet," Megan said to herself. She replied to his text:

I'm just kidding, Liam. Dinner is just fine.

Just then Laney poked her head in the door.

"Meeting's all set, and everyone will be in the conference room in 10 minutes."

"Oh wow, an hour went by that fast?" Megan asked surprised.

"It sure did. I'll see you in the meeting," Laney said and vanished from the doorway.

Bzzz Bzzz.

Megan's phone was vibrating again. It was another text from Liam.

39

Are you sure? Getting a masseuse is no
problem.

Megan was almost tempted. She could use a good massage, but she just wanted to spend time with Liam more than anything. She replied to his text.

I'm so sure. Dinner and time with my dear
friend are all I need.

Megan opened her top drawer, placed her phone in, closed the drawer and headed to the conference room.

Upon entering the conference room Megan was happy to see that eager faces were belonging to the people sitting at the table.

"Good morning team," Megan said. She walked over to her seat but remained standing. "I wanna cut right to the chase. Laney tells me that we are booked for Gashange's Gallery and we've scouted some new artists. The first order of business will be to contact those artists and schedule an appointment with them so that we can review their art. Laney will follow up with all of you regarding this. Lastly, I want all appointments scheduled by Monday. Are there any questions so far?"

"Uh yes," said Dana the company's marketing manager. "What if we can't get all the artists in for an appointment by Monday?"

"Do they know their art is being considered for display and auction at a prestigious art gallery?" Megan asked.

"Yes, ma'am," Dana replied.

"Well, there you have it. If they cannot make it by any means necessary, they simply weren't hungry enough. Got it?" Megan was stern but respectful.

"Yes ma'am," said Dana.

"Folks, please remember that I'm looking for starving artists. Although we specialize in freelancers and amateurs, I need them to be ready. We are giving them opportunities that normally don't come easy and they must be able to show that they really want this."

Megan was passionate about helping other artists. Her love for art was the driving force behind starting Stone Art Enterprises. Her mission has always been to help make it easier for fellow artists who wanted to make a living selling their artwork. Megan's company has made that possible by scouting raw talent on social media sites and posting ads for new artists to bring their work in to be evaluated. If the artists' work was found remarkable, Megan displayed their paintings or sculptures in her gallery. Eventually, special art expos were planned so the work could be sold. Because of Megan's company, the artists she chose were able to make at least three to five thousand dollars off one painting or sculpture sold. Of course, Megan's company charged a display fee and took a percentage from every piece sold.

"Are there any more questions?" Megan asked the team.

The room was silent, and Megan saw a few employees slowly shaking their heads.

Laney broke the silence. "I would like to add that 25 percent of the proceeds are going toward an art school in Compton."

"Compton? Why so far?" asked Mark who specialized in art appraisals.

Megan spoke up to answer his question.

"It's like I said before, guys. We wanna create opportunities for starving artists. This means expanding to inner-city communities and schools. There are lots of young artists out there as well. Can you imagine a teenage kid getting their art sold for $5000 or even $10,000? As crazy as it sounds, I've come across some awe-inspiring art by some very young people. Child prodigies are sometimes the best, and opportunities like this would blow their minds."

"Yeah, and it would be extremely encouraging for them," Laney added.

"Absolutely," said Megan. "They would be able to see that there's more to life than the negativity around them. Most importantly, they'd see that they can have a career in doing what they love the most."

"Sounds great to me," Dana agreed.

"Totally, expansion is good," said Mark.

"Great," said Megan. "I'm glad you guys are on board. Meeting is adjourned."

Megan left the conference room and went back to her office. Once she got there, she plopped down in her chair and reclined back. She closed her eyes and scanned her brain for what she should do next. Since Laney handled most of the day to day tasks, Megan often had to stop for a moment just to think of the next order of business.

Oh, that's right, she thought. She finally remembered something she needed to do. She opened the largest drawer on the right side of her desk where she kept her pocketbook. She leaned down and opened it just to grab a card from one of the side pockets.

The card had the number of the therapist Liam gave her. Megan looked at the card hesitantly, but then took a deep breath, picked up her office phone, and dialed the number.

A receptionist answered and Megan requested an appointment. After giving the receptionist the necessary information, Megan was scheduled for a visit a week from today. The thought made her nervous, but she thanked the receptionist and ended the call.

This is good, Megan, she thought. *You're doing everything you said you would.*

She opened the top drawer and grabbed her cell phone. She saw a text message from Liam.

Ok, see you at 6 p.m. then, dear friend;)

Megan chuckled at his text, then got back to work.

Chapter 5

Megan pulled up in front of Liam's luxury apartment building. She stepped out and gave the valet her keys.

"I'll take good care of her, ma'am," said the young valet.

"That's what I like to hear, thanks," Megan replied as she entered the building. She stopped at the front desk where the concierge paged Liam to let him know he had a visitor.

"You can go right up, ma'am," said the concierge politely.

"Thanks." Megan walked toward the elevator, pressed the button and the door opened instantly. She stepped onto the elevator and rode it up to Liam's 3-story penthouse. As she stepped off the elevator, a delightful aroma of seasonings and some type of meat being cooked graced her nostrils.

Oh, my goodness, she thought, *that smells amazing.* She knocked on the door and about 30 seconds later Liam came to open it.

"She finally made it," Liam teased. He flashed his handsome smile and leaned in to kiss her on the cheek.

"I could smell the food from the elevator," she said. "It smells even better in here. What you got cooking?"

"Follow me so I can show you."
Liam led the way to the kitchen. Once they made it to the kitchen, Megan was surprised to find a woman cooking. She gave Liam a puzzled look. He immediately took notice and spoke up.

"Megan, this is Shayla, my chef; and Shayla this is my good friend, Megan."

"Nice to meet you, Shayla," said Megan, not sure if she meant it.

"Nice to meet you too, Megan," Shayla said while quickly dicing a few green peppers and throwing them into a pot. "I'd shake your hand, but you know."

"It's totally fine, do your thing," Megan said smiling.

"Shayla's whipping up something special for you. You got filet mignon and lobster tail on the menu if you want it, and a whole bunch of other seafood

46

surprises, since I know you love seafood," Liam beamed.

"Aww thank you, Liam," Megan blushed.

"Let's go have a seat in the living room while Shayla finishes up."

"Let's do that," Megan agreed. She couldn't wait to find out what happened to his male chef. While there was nothing wrong with having a female chef, Megan took notice that Shayla wasn't *just* any female. She was quite beautiful with milk chocolate brown skin, a 5'9-inch voluptuous frame that had Megan's petite 5'6-inch frame beat, and a stylish short haircut that helped bring out her soft features.

As soon as Megan's behind hit Liam's soft leather couch she started in on him.

"So, what's up with Betty Crocker in there, huh?"

"What do you mean?" Liam asked naively.

Megan eyed him suspiciously. "Don't play dumb, Liam."

"Shayla's cooking for you. What's the problem?"

"The problem is she's not cooking for *me;* she's cooking for *you.* And tonight, I just wanted us to chill and just be us, you know?" Megan was undeniably being pouty. Liam rarely saw her get this way but was secretly amused when she did. He liked when she made him feel needed.

"Megan, everything's cool, sweetie. She's leaving after the food is done, alright?" He lifted his hand to brush away a few strands of hair out of her face. "You're looking pretty today."

"Thank you. I wanted to *look* how I felt," she said playfully.

"And I take it you felt like sunshine, huh?"

"Mmm, pretty much," Megan joked.

They laughed in unison and just that fast it became silent. Megan decided that Liam's answers regarding Shayla weren't satisfying enough so she inquired further about the mystery chef.

"I thought you had a male chef," she stated curiously.

"I do...well, I did. I mean, I still do but some things came up."

Megan raised a brow.

Liam continued. "My chef got sick and needed a little break."

"Okayyyy?" Megan said, waiting for further explanation.

"Shayla came highly recommended, so that's why she's here," Liam said honestly.

"So, she's your chef now until he gets better?"

"Yup, looks that way," Liam said as he got up and walked over to his wine bar. He grabbed a vintage bottle of wine along with two wine glasses and walked back to the couch.

"So enough about Shayla. How was your day?" He popped open the bottle with an electric corkscrew.

"It was actually pretty good. Very productive," Megan said feeling a bit excited.

"I'm glad to see you like this. It's like night and day compared to yesterday."

"I know," she admitted. "But thanks again for being there as brief as it was."

"You don't have to keep thanking me. How long have we known each other now?"

"About what?... Twelve years?"

"Yes. Freshmen year in college...well, your freshman year. I was already in my first year of med school."

"True. It's been a long time," Megan agreed.

"Exactly. Me being here for you is a given. So please stop thanking me." His tone was gentle as always.

"Well, that would be just rude, wouldn't it?" Megan teased.

Liam chuckled and poured some wine into Megan's glass, then into his. He then raised his glass.

"Let's make a toast," he said.

"To what?" Megan grabbed her glass.

"Uh, how 'bout to a productive day? Especially after a day like yesterday."

"That sounds good to me. Cheers to a productive day." They clinked their glasses together and each took a sip of their wine.

As they placed their glasses on the coffee table, Liam disapprovingly shook his head. "I don't know," he said. "Maybe toasting to that isn't enough. It's kind of corny. A productive day isn't anything new for you."

"Hmm, that is true," Megan said. She took a moment to think. "Let's see...oh, I got it!" she said with childlike excitement. Liam was all ears.

"I called the therapist today and made an appointment."

"You're lying," Liam said pleasantly surprised.

"Nope, my appointment is a week from today."

"That's incredible, Meg. I'm proud of you, woman." He playfully placed her in a headlock and gave her the world's softest noogie.

Megan laughed. "You better not mess up my hair, fool." She gave him a playful left uppercut to the gut.

"Okay, okay, whatever you say." He threw his hands up in surrender. Megan playfully kept her fist raised.

Liam smiled his gentle smile. "Seriously though, what are we toasting to now that you've made this big step?"

"Well, I guess there's only one thing we can toast to," Megan said.

"Okay, so go ahead, raise your glass," he said encouraging her.

"To change," she said with pride.

"That's perfect, Meg. Here's to change." Liam raised his glass.

"Here's to change," Megan repeated as she raised her glass as well.

"You've got some brighter days up ahead, Meg. Get excited."

"Oh, I am," she told him assuredly. "Especially since I've also decided to hire a private investigator to look into what happened to my father."

Liam's eyes widened. "You're just full of change tonight, huh?"

"I guess I am," she smiled mischievously.

"Well then, one last toast before we eat," said Liam.

"Let's do it."

51

"To Megha," he said raising his glass. "If it weren't for him, there'd be no you, Megan."

Megan was caught off guard at the mention of her father's name. However, she quickly snapped out of it when she realized this is exactly what she signed up for by agreeing to go to therapy. In therapy, there would be lots of things to catch her off guard and make her uncomfortable. Her best bet was to be ready with an opened mind and heart.

She smiled at Liam and raised her glass.

"To Megha, without him, there'd be no me."

Chapter 6

"Mom, would you stop worrying, please? Everything's gonna be fine, okay? I have to go or I'm gonna be late," Megan said into the phone. "Okay, I love you too. Bye." She hung up the phone and let out a stressful sigh. A few more minutes on the phone with her mother would've completely made her change her mind about therapy today.

Knock, knock. Laney stood in the doorway of Megan's office.

"Hey, Meg you got a minute before you go?"

"Sure, come on in," Megan said dryly.

"You okay?" Laney asked sensing that something was off.

Megan exhaled deeply. "It's just my mom. She...nothing, it's fine."

Laney realized that this was uncharted territory once Megan mentioned her mother. Still, she felt the

53

need to probe being that Megan came close to spilling the beans.

"I know you said that we should never discuss family issues, but Meg, we're friends for crying out loud. You can tell me...about anything, not just what's bothering you about your mom." The sincerity was evident in Laney's big green eyes.

Megan was touched. "I appreciate that, Laney. My mom's just driving me crazy, that's all." Megan paused for a moment, then continued. "She's trying to talk me out of going to therapy, even though she pretended to respect my wishes."

Laney looked puzzled. "You're going to therapy, boss lady?"

Megan gave Laney a cautionary look. "Right now, is not the time to be calling me *boss lady*, okay? I'm trying to confide in you."

"You're right. I'm sorry." Laney realized that Megan wasn't in a joking mood at all.

"It's okay. I'll just deal with it on my own," Megan said defeated.

"No, you don't deal with it on your own. You go to therapy, unleash all this negative energy and let *them* help you deal. That's what you're paying them for, right?"

Megan nodded. "You're absolutely right. Thanks, Laney, that was good advice," Megan said finally smiling.

"Anytime," Laney said. "Now back to business. I have the final files for the new artists we scouted. The team chose 15 artists out of the 23 original prospects. We just need you to make the final decision on whose work will be displayed at the event."

"Ok great. Is the art already in the showroom?" Megan asked.

"Yes, and here's the file for each piece," Laney said handing a folder to Megan.

"Awesome," Megan said taking the folder and placing it into her desk drawer. "I'll look at everything first thing in the morning. I've gotta go now, don't wanna be late for my first therapy session."

"Okay, I hope it goes well," Laney said as she exited Megan's office.

"Thanks," Megan yelled. Then she sighed and muttered: "I hope it goes well too."

She gathered her things and headed out the door.

When Megan arrived at the therapist's office the receptionist escorted her to a medium-sized room that didn't even come close to what Megan expected. For some reason, she imagined a boring looking office setting with the standard brown and wooden furniture. Instead, she was surprised by vibrant colors, fine art displayed on each wall, great natural lighting; compliments to the skylight, along with a calming lavender scent that filled the room, and the tranquil sounds of water flowing through an indoor fountain. Megan was highly impressed. She was also happy that the environment caused her to feel at ease, which she figured was the purpose anyway.

Just then a petite middle-aged woman came walking into the room.

"Well, hello, you must be Megan," she said. "I'm Dr. Tara Green, but you can call me Tara."

"Hi, nice to meet you, Dr. Green... I'd like to call you Dr. Green if that's okay," Megan said. She didn't want to call a woman who was old enough to be her mother by her first name.

"That's fine, hon," Dr. Green said giving Megan a warm smile. "Have a seat on the couch and let's get started."

Megan sat down as she was instructed and watched as Dr. Green took a seat in a chair stationed directly across from her. Megan was intrigued by Dr. Green's style and appearance. She was clearly a small woman standing at about 5'2 but her six-inch heels gave her an extra boost. She wore an off-shoulder retro-chic pink and black dress that complimented her light-skin tone. Megan also admired Dr. Green's curly shoulder-length mane with blonde high lights. Megan was impressed for the second time today and inspired by another successful black woman.

"First off I'd like to say thanks for making the decision to see a therapist. I know that therapy is not normally what *our* people like to get into, so I commend you on that."

"Thank you," Megan said politely.

"Second, I am not about to waste your time or mine, so let's get right into it, shall we?"

"Uh, sure...I, I don't really know where to start. This is all new to me," Megan admitted nervously.

"It's okay, don't be nervous. Why don't you take some deep breaths and then start by telling me why you wanted to see a therapist in the first place." Dr. Green's tone was soothing.

Megan did as she was told and before she knew it, she had babbled on for the whole hour with barely any feedback from Dr. Green.

Dr. Green's watch beeped, and she pressed the button to silence the alarm. "Well, that's our time for today, Megan."

"Really? That went by so fast," Megan said disappointed. "I hardly feel like you helped me."

"Well, how *do* you feel?" asked Dr. Green calmly.

"Like I just sat here telling you my life story while you just nodded. I feel... cheated," Megan said frustrated.

"Megan, I need you to trust the process, okay?"

"You don't even have a notebook," Megan said emphatically.

Dr. Green remained calm although she could see that Megan was increasingly getting flustered. "I remember everything you said, Megan. I don't need a notebook." She paused and examined Megan's expression which showed that she was still annoyed.

Dr. Green sighed softly. "I can't say much now, but you'll see that next time will be different, I promise."

Megan didn't know how to respond. She felt like she wasted her money, and her spirit was suddenly downcast.

Dr. Green looked at Megan and smiled mischievously. "Do you want to know a secret?"

"I guess," Megan said half interested.

"I don't use a notebook... because I have a recorder." Dr. Green laughed heartily. The revelation caught Megan off guard, but she slowly came around. She began to chuckle lightly, and before long she was cracking up.

Dr. Green's so-called secret wasn't that funny, but her laughter behind it was contagious. On top of that, Megan appreciated Dr. Green's attempt to lighten the mood. It made Megan feel much better and she was back to liking her.

"I'm sorry that I got upset," Megan said.

"Nothing I'm not used to," Dr. Green assured her. "I keep the recorder hidden through a built-in system because in the past visible recorders made things a little uneasy for some of my patients. My receptionist simply presses the record button as soon as I walk into the room."

"I understand, and thanks for explaining that, I know you didn't have to."

"I did what was necessary," Dr. Green stated. "I'd like you to come back in two days. Can you do that?"

Megan nodded. "I'm pretty sure I can."

"Good. I look forward to seeing you then. We've got a lot of ground to cover."

"Well, in that case, I'm excited," Megan said clasping her hands.

Dr. Green smiled, then stood to escort Megan out of the room.

Chapter 7

Two days later Megan was in her office talking on the phone with Liam and telling him about the therapy session. "I really can't say if it was beneficial so far. As I said, I was frustrated in the end."

"Okay, but you also said she made you feel a little better before you left, right?" Liam asked.

"Yeah, she did. That's why I'm going back today and hoping for a better outcome."

"You know you can't rush an outcome in therapy, right Meg?" He wanted Megan to understand that therapy was a process that would take time.

Megan huffed into the phone. "I guess," she said.

"Just try to relax," Liam coached. "Dr. Tara is great at what she does. My patients love her. I bet if you just let go and trust her *and* the process, you would love her too."

"Well I'll try my best," Megan said reluctantly. Liam couldn't help but laugh at Megan because he knew she wanted a quick fix.

"I have a patient in fifteen minutes and I wanna quickly go over this chart," Liam said.

"Okay, hold up. I need to ask you something," said Megan.

"What's that?"

"Don't call me stupid or anything, but are you sure I'm not seeing a psychiatrist? Because something is telling me that Dr. Green is a psychiatrist and I didn't agree to that."

Megan heard Liam sigh into the phone. "Okay, don't freak out, but yes, she is a psychiatrist," Liam admitted.

"Liam!" Megan yelled into the phone. Liam quickly responded before she went completely off on him.

"But she's also a licensed family therapist and she's not treating you as a patient with mental illness. So, chill out," he said.

"Fine, but I'm trusting you in this, Liam," Megan warned.

"I know, and I got you," he assured her. "So, like I said, chill...and look at it this way, you got one woman, plus two educations, which equals the best treatment for you."

"Okay, I guess you're right," Megan said, sounding more relaxed this time. "Talk to you later."

"Have a good session, sweetie. Call me later if necessary."

"Will do," said Megan and hung up the phone. She didn't know why she was making a big deal out of Dr. Green being a psychiatrist. However, a part of her realized it was because she didn't want to feel like she needed help when it came to her mental status. Yet another part of her consistently came up with excuses not to go to therapy, no matter how many times she'd successfully convinced herself that she needed it. Regardless of how Megan felt, she mustered up the courage to go and was determined to stick it out. She grabbed her purse and car keys and left the office.

"It's good to see you again, Megan," Dr. Green said as she strolled into the room. Megan was sitting comfortably on Dr. Green's purple velvet couch but slightly anxious about how today's session would go.

"Thanks," Megan replied. "Good to see you too."

"Let's get started," Dr. Green said as she sat in her chair.

Megan sat up straight, still nervous but ready to dive in.

"I went over the recording of our first session and collected lots of information that I'd like to go over today. Just so you know, the recording has since been deleted for confidential purposes, and a new one has been started for this session."

Megan gave a nod of approval and Dr. Green continued.

"So, as you know, you gave me tons of information the last time you were here. It might've been the first time I've ever learned so much from a person in one sitting."

"Is that a good thing?" Megan asked.

"Oh yes. It's very good. In fact, I already have some recommendations for you before you leave here today."

"Great," Megan said. She could feel herself starting to ease up.

"The strategy I use to get people to open up doesn't always work as quickly as it has with you. This lets me know you had a lot of things building up inside."

"Yeah, I have," Megan agreed.

"Was there no one else at all you could talk to?"

"No, not really. The only person who would ever listen is my friend, Liam."

"And somehow you thought that wasn't good enough, correct?"

"Well, I-

"If you thought it was good enough, you wouldn't be here. Don't you think?" Dr. Green said, interrupting Megan to get her to think before she answered.

"I guess you could say that. But I do appreciate everything Liam has done for me. It's just that he wasn't there that day, so he doesn't understand." Megan almost felt bad for saying anything less than good about her friend.

"Don't be so hard on yourself," Dr. Green said as if she could read Megan's mind. "Who was there that you've tried to talk to but couldn't?"

"My mother. She witnessed everything just like I did. My brother was there too, but he says he can't remember anything. I guess he was too young." Megan began to stare blankly.

"Stay with me, Megan," Dr. Green said waving her hands.

"Sorry," Megan said snapping out of it.

"Megan, how is your relationship with your mother? As I listened to the recording it sounds as if you are angry with her. Tell me why."

"When I was a kid, my mother and brother were all I had after my father was taken. But as an adult, I learned to resent my mother."

"What do you mean *learned* to resent her?" Dr. Green said curiously.

"Well as a child I never understood why she did certain things, but as I got older, those things she did in the past angered me and I became resentful toward her."

"What things are you speaking of?"

"Well for starters, she married my father's best friend shortly after my father was taken."

This revelation took Dr. Green by surprise, but she maintained her composure and proceeded with her questions.

"How soon after your father disappeared did your mother marry his best friend?"

"I don't know, four or five months."

"Is she still married to him?"

"No, she's not. She's actually on her fourth husband now," Megan said, disgusted.

"I take it the resentment is still there?" Dr. Green asked.

"Yes," Megan said without hesitation.

"Okay. This changes a few things though. Before we started, I planned on sending you out with a couple of recommendations that I now feel we should hold off on."

Megan gave Dr. Green a disapproving glare. Dr. Green took notice as always.

"Trust the process, remember?" she said to Megan.

Megan nodded concededly.

"I have a new recommendation. I want you to confront your mother."

"Confront her about what?" Megan asked.

"Excuse me, *confront* isn't the right word. I want you to simply have a talk with her and tell her how you feel about her marrying your father's best friend."

"There will be nothing simple about that conversation, trust me. And I'm not doing it."

"Well don't you at least want to know why she did it?"

"Of course I do, but you don't know my mother. She won't talk about anything that has to do with the past. It's like she erases the years from her mind as she goes along." Megan was becoming irritated, not so much with Dr. Green but by the notion itself.

"I understand that this could be hard, but it is an exercise that will bring you closure and help start the healing process."

"No, I won't do it. It's pointless," Megan said adamantly.

"Fine," Dr. Green said softly. "How about your father's best friend then? Is he still around?"

"Yeah, but I haven't spoken to him in years. I wouldn't even know how to begin."

"You could begin by being honest. Invite him somewhere to talk, have lunch... I don't know. Just let him know that you need answers concerning your father and you can't think of anyone better to give them to you. How's that?"

"So, you're saying to get him to talk about my father and then ask him why he married my mother?"

"Bingo!" Dr. Green said excitingly.

Megan sighed deeply. "I think I can do that."

"Great," Dr. Green said smiling. "We'll talk about it during our next session, so act fast."

Chapter 8

Megan set out for her morning jog, this time with her brother, Kent, to keep her company.

"I'm glad you came out with me today," Megan told her brother. "I've missed this."

"I'm glad too. I'm sorry I've been MIA," said Kent.

"It's okay, we both have busy lives, so I understand."

"Mom says you've been seeing a shrink."

"Seriously, Kent? A *shrink?* Don't do that?" Megan didn't appreciate her brother's free use of the word one bit.

"What?" Kent said naively.

"I'm seeing a therapist, okay? Not a *shrink*, so cut it out."

"Alright, don't shoot the messenger."

"So that's what mom's telling people? That I'm seeing a shrink?"

Kent nodded.

"Unbelievable," Megan said bitterly.

Kent shrugged. "You know how she is, so why you trippin'?

"Because it gets tiring," Megan snapped.

"Yooo, Sis...calm down alright?" Kent said, trying to steer the conversation in a positive direction. "Do you think I came up here to argue with you? I came to have a nice morning run with you for old times' sake, that's it."

"I'm sorry. I'm not trying to take it out on you. I just have a lot on my mind, bro," Megan admitted.

It had almost been a week since Megan's last session with Dr. Green and she avoided going back simply because she didn't have the courage to call Stan, her former stepfather and father's best friend.

"You could talk to me too you know? I'm not a shri— Kent caught himself before letting the word slip. "I mean... a therapist, but I listen."

Megan playfully scowled at him. "Well, since you offered; my therapist wants me to confront Uncle Stan about marrying mom, and I'm terrified to reach out to him."

"Interesting...but why are you scared? Uncle Stan was always cool," Kent said confused.

"I guess I'm afraid of his answers. I honestly don't know why I'm afraid, but I am," Megan said.

"I say just do it," Kent said as if it was the easiest thing in the world.

"When was the last time you spoke to him?" Megan asked.

"About a month ago... something like that."

"Exactly. That's why it's so easy for you to tell me to call him. Unlike you I haven't spoken to him in years," Megan confessed.

"Well dang. Why not?" Kent asked, puzzled.

"Why should I? Why should *you?* He married his best friend's wife. A man like that can't be trusted."

Kent let Megan's words sit for a moment before he spoke. Then he said: "What you're saying makes a lot of sense. But Stan is the closest thing I have to a father figure, so it's harder for me to see it your way."

"I respect that. Now let's start this jog," Megan said and took off with Kent jogging closely behind.

They made their way up the mountainside where the hill was a bit narrow, keeping them one behind the other. As they jogged, they could hear the rustling of leaves blowing in the breeze. It was a perfect day for running and they didn't have to worry about the heat causing them to cut the run short. As they ran further up the hill, the path widened, allowing them to jog side by side.

"Are you coming to my event at Gashange's?" Megan asked.

"Yeah, I could swing by. It's in a few days, right?"

"Yup, as if I don't already have enough going on," Megan said half playfully.

"Yeah but this is work. You love work," Kent said as if to remind her.

"True."

"You excited?"

"I'm trying to be. Believe me, I am."

"Well, try to focus on the good things you got going on, you know? You can deal with that other stuff later."

Megan nodded, but Kent could see that she was still thinking too hard. He abruptly stopped jogging and gently gripped her arm prompting her to stop as well.

"I'll tell you what, when you call Uncle Stan, I'll go with you. Will that help?"

Megan's eyes brightened. "Oh my goodness, thank you!" she said as she hugged her brother tightly.

"Of course, I got your back," Kent said assuredly.

Megan smiled, but her smile quickly faded when she heard a strange sound coming from the trees. "Do you hear that?"

72

Kent stopped to listen but heard nothing.

"Don't be paranoid, Sis," he said nonchalantly.

"I'm not. I just heard something."

"It's nothi-

Before Kent could finish, a large mountain lion leaped down from the mountainside onto his back. The lion used its strength to bring Kent to the ground and didn't waste any time sinking its teeth in. Kent let out a painful shout as Megan looked on in horror. Fortunately, Kent managed to get his arms up to block his face and neck, leaving only his arms to be bitten. As Kent squirmed and tried to protect himself, Megan finally snapped out of it and looked for something to fight the creature off. By the time she found a thick sturdy branch, the lion gave up on biting Kent's arms and settled for his left thigh. Kent screamed in agony as the mountain lion's fangs pierced through his femoral artery causing blood to squirt from the puncture site.

Megan ran over to the lion and swung the branch as hard as she could, hitting it in the head. The first hit only seemed to stagger the beast but didn't keep it from attacking Kent. Megan forcefully swung the branch and struck the mountain lion in the head two more times. This time the animal collapsed over Kent's legs. Seeing that the lion wasn't moving, Megan remembered that she had a pocketknife in her fanny pack. She pulled the knife out and drove it into the center of its throat. The first time was tough, so she did it twice more. When she was convinced the beast was dead, she grabbed it by its hind legs and pulled it off Kent.

What next? Megan thought anxiously. Instantly, she remembered a lifesaving trick Liam taught her years ago during his medical residency. She quickly removed Kent's sneakers, then his socks. She tied both socks together, making them long enough to act as a tourniquet, then tied it above Kent's puncture wound. Kent groaned in pain.

"It's okay, brother. I'm here," she said soothingly.

Megan then reached into her fanny pack for her cell phone and dialed 911. She told the operator their approximate location, and the operator let her know that assistance would be there as soon as possible.

After Megan placed the 911 call, she called Liam for back up. She was scared out of her mind but put on a brave face for Kent.

"The ambulance should be here soon, Kent. You're gonna be okay."

Megan looked around anxiously. She was worried that another mountain lion would appear and hoped the ambulance would arrive soon.

Chapter 9

Megan nervously paced back and forth in the hospital's emergency waiting room as the doctors worked on Kent. She called her mother but there was no answer, so she left her a message. She was happy that Liam was on his way so she could have some type of moral support. Plus, she needed someone to help keep her calm.

Megan finally decided to sit down, but instead of pacing, she rocked back and forth. Her mind wasn't in a good space. The incident with Kent reminded Megan of her childhood trauma and she was back to being a scared little girl. Although she was hopeful that Kent would be alright, the thought of things taking a turn for the worse tortured her soul. Megan was trying her hardest to keep it together, but she felt like she was on the verge of a meltdown.

"Megan!" She heard a familiar voice call from a short distance. She looked to her right where the voice was coming from and was relieved to see Liam running down the hall. Megan quickly stood to embrace him.

"Thank God you're here. I wasn't sure how long I had before I lost it."

"How is he? What are they saying?" Liam appeared calm, but Megan knew he was trying to hide the fact that he was nervous as well. She knew how much Liam had grown to love Kent as his own little brother.

"They took him back for emergency surgery," she informed him. "That was about 30 minutes ago, and I haven't heard anything since."

"Well, that sounds about right," Liam said. "I guess we'll just have to wait." He gently led Megan back over to the row of chairs to sit down.

"Were you able to get in contact with your mother?"

Megan shook her head. "I left her a brief message. I didn't want to text her something like this but she's taking a little longer than usual to respond, so maybe I might have to."

"Yeah, that's a tough one," agreed Liam. "I'm not sure what to tell you about that."

There was an awkward pause, then Liam interrupted it.

"Megan, don't take this the wrong way but how many times have I told you that you shouldn't go jogging in the mountains?"

Megan sighed. She didn't have the strength to respond even though she wanted to defend herself. Undoubtedly, she despised the question since it almost confirmed that what happened to Kent was her fault. Still, she wished she could tell Liam how brave she was; how she defended her brother against the fearsome animal and drove her knife through its throat. But what point would that prove? Kent wasn't out of the woods yet, and Liam would only respond by letting her know that her bravery would never have been necessary if she had only heeded his warning in the first place.

After realizing that he wasn't going to get an answer, Liam spoke again.

"I'm sorry. I shouldn't have brought that up, especially at this time," he said remorsefully.

"It's okay. You have a right to feel some type of anger, I guess."

"I'm not angry, Megan. I just-

"Wished I would've listened to you?" she said, blandly finishing his statement.

Liam could see the sadness in Megan's eyes. The expression on her face was guilt-ridden and he knew it was time to change the subject.

"He's gonna be alright, you'll see. And don't worry, this is not your fault, okay?" He patted her on the thigh and gave her a compassionate smile.

Megan nodded. She took hold of his hand and gave it a tight squeeze. "You know I don't normally do this, but can you pray with me, Liam?"

"Of course," Liam replied. He was shocked by her request but quickly tried to hide it. He grew up in a Christian household and carried those values into adulthood. Megan often saw how dedicated Liam was to his prayer life and going to church every Sunday. As a woman who didn't grow up in a religious or spiritual home, Megan wasn't used to praying or much less the mention of God. For this reason, she always took Liam's Christian lifestyle lightly. Although she believed there was a God, she hardly spoke to Him. However, for some strange reason, she felt a nudging deep within to pray. She knew she didn't know exactly how to pray so she asked Liam to do it for her.

Liam knew that Megan asking him to pray with her was a huge deal. He saw the seriousness of the question as he watched Megan bow her head. With that, he asked no further questions, grabbed both her hands and begin praying for Kent.

A few moments after Liam finished praying a doctor came walking toward them. Megan grew anxious as the doctor came closer. He looked to be about 5'10, had a medium built and a bald head. His appearance was welcoming, and his brown skin was free of wrinkles although it was clear that he was over the age of 55.

"Hi there. My name's Dr. Nash, head of the vascular surgery department. You're here for Kent Stone, correct?" He darted his eyes from Megan to Liam, then back to Megan.

"Yes, I'm his sister. How is he?" Megan asked nervously.

"Well, thankfully the bites on his arms were minor, so we just cleaned and wrapped them up. But we had to stitch the puncture to his femoral artery, which was successful. However, he's lost lots of blood, to the point where he needs an emergency transfusion."

"Oh no, does that mean he won't make it if he doesn't get it?" Megan was beginning to panic.

"It's going to be okay," Dr. Nash assured her. "We're searching for a donor now, but we wanted to talk to you first to see if you were a match and if so, we hoped you'd want to be a donor for your brother."

"Most definitely. Let's do it." Megan was ready to give her life for Kent if she had to.

"Great. First, we're going to need your blood type. Do you happen to know it offhand?" Asked Dr. Nash.

"Um, I think it's A positive or something. I'm not sure. I'm sorry, I knew back in college." Megan felt embarrassed.

"It's okay, Meg, lots of people don't know their blood type," Liam said trying to make Megan feel better.

"That's correct," agreed Dr. Nash. "And no worries because we can find out right now. Follow me so we can get your blood drawn and sent to the lab ASAP."

Megan and Liam followed Dr. Nash down the hall, through a pair of double doors, and into a blood drawing station.

"You can have a seat in the chair right there," Dr. Nash said to Megan. "I'll have a nurse tend to you right away."

Megan did as she was told and watched as Dr. Nash approached a tall, strong, and athletic-looking nurse at the nurse's station. He said a few inaudible words then walked away. Shortly after Dr. Nash left the nurse's station, the amazon nurse made her way toward Megan. She looked to be about 40 years old, with dark brown hair, blue eyes, and pale skin.

"Good morning, I'm Sadie and I'll be taking your blood." The nurse was polite, but Megan could tell Sadie didn't want to waste any time.

Nurse Sadie went to wash her hands and gather all the supplies needed to draw Megan's blood.

"You're doing a great thing for your brother," Sadie said as she applied a tourniquet around Megan's left arm.

"Thanks. I just want him to be okay," Megan said.

"I understand, but he'll be fine. Dr. Nash is exceptional and very thorough," Sadie said as she cleaned the crease of Megan's forearm with an alcohol prep pad.

Megan was happy to hear this and started to feel at ease. Before she knew it, Sadie was telling her to apply pressure to the venipuncture as she labeled the tube.

"Okay, we're all set. Would you like a band-aid?

"No thanks," said Megan.

"Okay then. I'm going to bring this down to the lab, so we can get those results ASAP. I hope all goes well, and it was nice meeting you," said Nurse Sadie.

"Thank you, same here," replied Megan. "Can we go back to the waiting room?"

"Sure, just follow the path in the same direction you came from."

As Nurse Sadie left, Liam and Megan exited the drawing station and made their way back to the waiting area.

"Why didn't you get a band-aid?" Liam asked.

"Wow, you're still here, huh?" Megan joked. "You've been quiet the whole time."

Liam smiled. He was glad to see that Megan was lightening up. "What was I supposed to say?"

"I don't know. You're a doctor. You could've said anything."

"I don't need to tell another doctor how to do his or her job. Besides, if it was done to me, I'd hate it, so I don't do it. I try to live by the Golden Rule."

"I guess that makes sense," Megan said.

"Don't worry. If I sense a doctor isn't doing everything they can, I'm definitely gonna speak up. But you should've taken that band-aid though."

"Oh my gosh, it's not a big deal," Megan said half smiling. "I just hate taking them off."

"Yeah well, we're in a hospital and even that little puncture needs to be protected."

Megan playfully rolled her eyes and gave Liam a look that said, "*oh please.*"

"This is where most infections are acquired, lady," Liam said, reading her face accurately.

"Oh, so now you wanna be my doctor," Megan said sarcastically.

"Hey, I'm just stating the facts."

They made it to the waiting room and took their seats.

◻◻◻◻◻◻◻◻◻

About 20 minutes later, Dr. Nash came walking down the hall again. Megan could tell that something wasn't quite right.

"Hi Megan," said Dr. Nash. "I have to cut to the chase for the sake of time. Unfortunately, you weren't a match for your brother. He has O negative blood and your blood type is AB positive."

"What? I don't understand. What does that mean?" Megan was on the verge of tears.

"It just means you can't be a donor. Your brother, on the other hand, can donate to you if ever needed, but *he* can only receive O negative blood."

"I still don't understand. I-

"It's okay," Liam interrupted. "Dr. Nash, I'm Dr. Franklin, internal medicine. I'll explain it to her later. Please go forward with your back up plan."

Dr. Nash gave Liam a respectful Nod. "I reached out to another hospital and had them send over O negative blood just in case you weren't a match. While the lab was testing your blood, I also had the O negative blood retested and everything is clear. So, we're going to do the transfusion now and your brother will be just fine."

Megan was still a bit shaken and could only manage to nod, so Liam spoke on her behalf.

"Sounds great, Doctor. Thanks for being so thorough."

"It's no problem. I wouldn't have it any other way," Dr. Nash said smiling. "I'll let you know when the procedure is done."

"We'll be here," said Liam.

Dr. Nash disappeared down the hall again and Liam let out a sigh of relief.

"Thank you, Jesus!" he said.

However, he quickly noticed that Megan didn't seem to share his relief.

"Megan, sweetie, this is great news. Kent is going to be alright. Why are you still pouting?"

"I- I'm sorry. I know I shouldn't be. I'm just confused as to why I wasn't a match. I'm his sister."

"Meg, you're reading way too deep into this. Siblings aren't always a match. The blood type depends on the parents. Both their blood types together determine their children's, and sometimes the kids don't get the same types. It's all good. I mean, what are you thinking here?" Liam tried to comfort Megan, but he was confused as to why she chose to dwell on the blood types instead of rejoicing over her brother getting a match.

"I don't know," was all she could say.

Chapter 10

The next day Megan rolled out of bed with nothing but yesterday's incident on her mind. She was relieved that Kent survived the attack and was able to get a match for his blood transfusion. However, she couldn't get the fact that they weren't a match out of her head. Even though Liam told her it wasn't a big deal and it meant nothing, she wasn't so sure.

Although she didn't have time to be concerned with her woes, her anxiety on the matter wouldn't let up and she needed answers. That's why she set up a meeting with her mother's ex-husband and father's ex-best friend, Stan.

She took the fastest shower ever, got dressed, and threw her hair into a ponytail. She did a once over in the mirror and felt she didn't look the greatest. A second set of eyes would have begged to differ as Megan was a natural beauty who couldn't look bad if she tried. But who was she kidding anyway? It was Uncle Stan and being that she had no respect for the man, she most certainly couldn't care less about how she appeared to him.

The event at Gashange's was now two days away and Megan knew that she shouldn't have been concerned with much else. However, a conversation with Uncle Stan was long overdue, especially after yesterday. So, she gathered her bearings, took a deep breath, grabbed her car keys and purse, and headed out the door.

Megan parked her car in the parking lot of an outside Bistro. The sun was out and there was a calming breeze. She stepped out of her car and walked down the pathway toward the table where she saw Stan sitting. Her heart began to beat rapidly as she got closer to him, so she took a few deep breaths to settle herself.

As she approached the table, Stan noticed her and stood as a courtesy.

Megan, good morning," he said smiling. He walked over to her chair to pull it out for her.

"Thank you," Megan said. She barely smiled at him, yet she appreciated his chivalry.

"No problem," Stan said, retaking his seat. "The waiter was here already but I told him to come back in about five minutes."

Megan nodded. She wasn't sure what to say or how to start. One thing she knew for sure was that she wasn't there to fraternize with Uncle Stan, let alone break bread with the man. She wanted to get this talk over with.

Stan could feel that the energy between him and Megan was more than awkward, so he attempted to break the ice.

"So, how have you been? I heard some great things about you through Kent."

"Things have been great, actually. At least businesswise they have." Megan's response was uninviting. A thing Stan took notice of. Her tone was impatient, but he was relentless.

"Is there something else troubling you?"

"Uh, yeah. Lots of things," she said sarcastically.

Stan sighed. He was trying, but it was evident that Megan just wasn't into having small talk. The truth is, Stan Hopkins was not the kind of man to beat around the bush. However, for the love of his late best friend, and Megan once being his stepdaughter, he thought it was best to try easing into things by starting off being as friendly as possible. After all, he had nothing against Megan, but he could see by her attitude and body language that she couldn't say the same when it came to him. So, he finally did them both a favor and relented.

"Okay, Megan, why did you want to meet with me today?"

Megan was caught off guard and wasn't ready to answer, so she froze.

"It's okay, just come out with it," Stan said. "I know we don't have the best relationship because you've grown angry toward me, but I have always loved you. Believe it or not." He was trying to be both comforting and encouraging.

Megan looked confused. "How did you know I had anger toward you?"

Stan chuckled lightly. "Sweetheart, I saw the love you once had for me leave your eyes little by little each day while I was married to your mother. I mean, at first you seemed okay, but when it started to fade, I noticed...and it hurt. But a man's gotta do what he's gotta do."

"Are you kidding me?" Megan said incredulously. "So, you think that marrying your best friend's wife was dignified?" She was disgusted.

"Well, yes," Stan said calmly. "As weird as it may seem to others, I had my reasons."

At this point Megan didn't know what to say or do, so she let her anger control her portion of the conversation.

"It wasn't weird, okay? It was wrong. It's wrong to conspire against your friend, have an affair with his wife then have a secret love child and make my father think that Kent was his. That's wrong!" Megan's eyes welled up with tears. Her emotions were all over the place and they forced her to come to her own conclusions without any proof on the matter.

Stan looked at Megan in total bewilderment. However, he quickly gained his composure to address her accusations.

"Megan, I don't understand where all of this is coming from, love. These are honestly some serious allegations."

"So, are you trying to say that they're not true?" Megan tried to gain control of her rattled nerves.

"I'm not *trying* to say anything. I'm telling you that none of that is true. I would never hurt your father like that. You clearly don't know how much I loved that man." Stan loosened his tie and tried not to get choked up.

While Stan fought to hide his emotions, Megan saw nothing but sorrow in his eyes. Seeing this caused her to back down and she decided to ask her questions with a bit more compassion.

"Well, if you loved him so much, why would you marry his wife?"

"I was trying to do the right thing by him. The money that he left for you and your brother only secured your future, but there wasn't enough money for you guys to make it through that present time."

"What about the money from his businesses? Couldn't we have lived off that?" Megan asked.

"That's what we thought at first, but something shady went on with all your father's businesses shortly after his abduction. For some reason, the money was gone...from all his accounts."

Megan shifted in her seat. She suddenly felt nauseous and her ears were on fire. *Can I really do this?* she thought. *Do I really wanna hear this?*

Stan noticed Megan's discomfort but continued. "It's possible that the men who took him forced him to clean out all his bank accounts and hand the money over. After that, there's no telling what they did to him. I just wish there were a body, so we could give him the proper burial and have some closure."

"Me too," Megan said as she fought back tears. There was a moment of somber silence. The waiter appeared shortly afterward, and they were both relieved to see him. He politely took their orders and went on his way. Stan took the opportunity to look Megan in the eyes. He reached across the table and gently took hold of her hands.

"Listen, I knew that if I didn't step in, your mother would've eventually had to use the trust funds your father worked so hard to secure. I just couldn't let that happen. So yeah, I honored the man, my friend, and my brother, by marrying his wife. I wanted to make sure that all of his family's needs and wants were met. For that, I have no regrets."

Megan was almost at a loss for words. She had accused the man of betraying her father without fully knowing his reasoning for his actions. Megan could see that Stan's words were sincere and she felt terrible for the hate and anger she had toward him over the years. Yet, there were still some things she didn't understand and questions that remained unanswered.

"Uncle Stan, this is a lot to take in, almost too much. I'm still so confused about Kent?"

"What about Kent?" Stan raised a brow.

Megan went on to explain everything that happened yesterday, including why she has come to question Kent's paternity.

"Wow, Meg. I don't know what to say about that," Stan said, surprised by Megan's new-found suspicions. "First off, let me say I'm glad Kent is alright. I'll have to go see him for sure. Second, once again these are wild accusations and assumptions that your father would've been heartbroken by. He never once questioned Kent being his."

"So, you're saying there's no way you're Kent's father, right?" Megan wanted to be sure she covered all the possibilities.

"I'm positive. And you wanna know something else?"

"What?" Megan was all ears.

"You're not gonna believe this, but Keres and I never had sex...ever."

"What?... You're kidding, right?" Megan shook her head in disbelief. "That's impossible."

"Not for us it wasn't," Stan assured her. "When I came to your mother with the idea of marriage, I let it be known that it was to be strictly platonic and that it was only for business purposes. She was fine with that. Besides, this was my best friend's wife and I didn't look at her like that."

"So, what did you guys do, have sex with *other* people?"

"Exactly. I had a few flings at first, but then I started dating a woman that I began to fall for. She knew all about the marriage arrangement with Keres, but as our relationship grew, she wanted more of me. For her, more of me meant *all* of me."

"So, what did you do? Did you have to dump her?"

Stan chuckled. "No, sweetheart. I asked Keres for a divorce with the promise of alimony until she got re-married. She happily signed the papers."

"Whoa, so that's how it ended, huh?"

"*How* and *why* it ended. I married the love of my life and still kept my word in providing for Megha's family."

"Wait, so your wife Jasmine, was the woman you fell for back then?"

"Yes indeed. And she's still my everything. On top of that, she's very supportive of my relationship with Kent. She knows how important Megha was to me and that I'd do anything for his kids...that means you too, Megan."

She smiled at Stan for the first time in decades.

"I'm so sorry for how I've misjudged you over the years. If I'd only asked these questions sooner, I could've given you the respect you've always deserved. Instead, I shut you out, thinking I knew everything. Can you please forgive me, Uncle Stan?" Megan was truly remorseful and felt like a fool.

"Megan, you were a child who went through a traumatic situation. Life was changing fast for you and no one bothered to explain anything. I get why you were angry. It's my fault for not coming to you to explain my position once you got old enough to understand."

"Uncle Stan, it's okay. I appreciate what you did for us. Just please forgive me for my unwarranted hate and anger toward you." Her eyes were pleading with his.

Stan smiled warmly. "All is forgiven, love." He stood and walked toward Megan and the two shared a loving embrace.

Just then the waiter approached with their food.

"Ahh, right on time. Now let's eat and put all of this behind us," Stan said joyously.

"Sounds good to me," Megan said, feeling lighter.

"Meg, can I say one more thing?"

"Sure." Megan took a sip of her water.

"I'm happy that we were able to reconcile today. But I'm afraid that you're looking too deep into this situation with Kent. Your brother may look just like Keres, but he's your father all the way. He has his mannerisms and everything. It amazes me how much they are alike. I don't think your suspicions are necessary. You should leave it alone, love.

Megan nodded. "I guess you're right."

Chapter 11

Megan stood in front of the full-length mirror in her bedroom. Her hair had been straightened to perfection the day before by her beautician, but today she added the finishing touches with a few loose curls for extra body. Megan also pinned the front left side of her hair up with a diamond-encrusted hair comb. She wore a black mermaid cut gown that had black lace long sleeves. She used her mother's Taylor to design her dress and was happy that he added the lace to help pull off the sexy but classy look she was going for. On top of that, the dress fit her like a glove and accentuated her curves. She wasn't as voluptuous as Shayla, but her shapely figure was just right for her petite size.

It was the day of her big event at Gashange's and although she was nervous, she was also extremely excited. Still, her excitement was bittersweet since

Kent, who was supposed to be her date, was still recovering in the hospital.

Megan smoothed her hands over the sides of her dress and gave herself a once over. Seeing that she was satisfied with her look, she blew a kiss to her reflection in the mirror. "You got this, girl."

She loved to give herself a brief affirmation before every event. The businesswoman in Megan revealed her more confident side, and she wasn't as timid as her mother believed. She grabbed her purse and keys, shut off all the lights in her house and left for the office where Laney was waiting to be picked up.

About twenty minutes later, Megan pulled up to the front of Stone Art Enterprises and called Laney on her cell phone to come outside.

Laney came out just moments later. Megan was impressed with Laney's appearance as she sauntered her way to the car. Laney's red hair was pulled back into a messy bun dressed in baby's breath, and she wore an emerald green cocktail dress with yellow pumps. Laney wasn't much of a fashionista, but Megan thought she looked classy enough for their event. Besides, not everyone had a mother like Keres who relentlessly stressed the importance of style.

"Hey, Meg." Laney carefully got into the passenger seat and closed the door.

"Hey, girl. Are you ready to do this?"

"As ready as I'll ever be," Laney said buckling her seatbelt. "The team has everything set up so nicely. You're gonna love it."

"That's what I like to hear," Megan said pulling off.

"So how are things going with Kent?"

"He's doing better. They're going to run a few more tests and if all goes well, he should be able to go home in two days."

"That's good. I know that whole ordeal had to be scary."

"Terrifying," Megan emphasized.

"It's too bad he couldn't be here, but he'd be proud of you."

"Thanks, Laney. I'm going to Facetime him later before we get started." Megan knew seeing her brother's face would help her feel better. She also knew she had no time to be missing him and being sentimental about it. It was time to put her game face on. More importantly, it was time for her to get Laney to drop the subject.

"So, we have everything set with the appraisals, right?" Megan asked with her eyes on the road.

"Yes, everything's all good. Mark even added four more appraisals for the paintings you didn't choose."

"And why would he do that if I've already made my choices of what's to be displayed and auctioned off?"

"Well, we figured that since you chose eleven out of the fifteen pieces, it wouldn't hurt to appraise the remnants. Just in case, you know?"

Megan thought for a moment. She realized it wasn't a bad idea. If the art expo went as well as planned, there may be room to auction off a few more paintings.

"Well, that's why I have a team, so I don't have to do all the thinking."

Laney smiled, glad that the idea pleased Megan.

Before they knew it, they were pulling into the parking lot of the Gashange's Gallery. They got out of the car and Megan handed her keys to the valet.

"Please be careful with my baby." The valet noticed that Megan's polite tone did not match her stern facial expression.

He respectfully nodded, then got into the car to find a parking space.

As Megan and Laney entered the gallery, the first thing they noticed was how packed it was. People were all over the place socializing, admiring the art, and sipping their drink of choice.

As Megan looked around, she noticed that the art pieces on the walls were outstanding, and the sculptures even more so. She knew that having an event here was a big deal but seeing such fine art confirmed that Gashange's only affiliated with the best of the best. It also made her more nervous, seeing that she had some big shoes to fill with the current displays.

Suddenly, a man approached her from behind. He tapped her gently on her shoulder and smiled when she turned to him.

"You must be Ms. Megan Stone."

"Yes, and you are?"

"I'm Melvin, the event coordinator for Gashange's." He held his hand out for Megan to shake. She smiled graciously upon shaking it. He was a short Latino man with a small frame, and only an inch taller than she was. His brown eyes were kind and put Megan at ease.

"It's a pleasure to meet you, Melvin."

"We are all very excited to be meeting *you*. Gashange's prides itself in appreciating fine and rare art, and you have developed quite a reputation for both."

Megan blushed.

"We are going to get started soon. Your paintings are in the great ballroom, where the auction will be held as well."

"Great. I can't wait," was all Megan managed to say. Melvin's welcome helped ease her nerves, but she still had butterflies. *Where did Laney go,* she thought. She scanned the gallery for Laney and spotted her talking to one of the guests.

"Will you excuse me, Melvin? I have to touch base with my assistant."

"Sure. I will be making the announcement soon so don't go too far," Melvin said.

"Got it." Megan began walking over to where Laney stood talking to a middle-aged Caucasian man with a short blonde haircut and side part. Before Megan could get to Laney, someone gently grabbed her arm. She looked at the hand and then up at the person it belonged to. Her face lit up instantly when she saw that it was Liam.

"You made it," Megan said taking hold of Liam's hands.

"Of course I made it." Liam brought Megan's hands up to his mouth and kissed them.

"Ahem." A woman suddenly appeared from behind Liam.

Megan's smile faded just as quickly as the woman had appeared. Attentive as usual, Liam became aware of Megan's sudden change in demeanor and went in for quick damage control.

"Megan, you remember Shayla, right?"

Megan feigned a smile and hardly nodded. "I remember. Your chef, right?"

Liam could sense a hint of sarcasm in Megan's tone. "Yes, but tonight she's my date."

"Well, it's nice to see you again, Shayla."

"Same here. I can't wait to see all the art," Shayla said.

Before Megan could give another phony response, she heard Melvin's voice come through a loudspeaker.

"Attention ladies and gentlemen. We are now opening the doors for tonight's event. Please proceed straight ahead to the great ballroom and let the auctioning begin!" Melvin's excitement caused the guests to clap and cheer.

Megan, on the other hand, was thankful for the timely delivery of his announcement. It was the perfect excuse to get away from Liam and Shayla.

"That's my cue. I'll see you guys inside," Megan said walking off and heading toward the great ballroom. As she entered the ballroom she was immediately overwhelmed by the room's stunning layout. The décor made Megan feel as if she was in a fairy tale. Everything sparkled and shined and the amount of gold in the room was mesmerizing. The cathedral ceiling was covered in hand-painted art, and some of the paint added a 3-dimensional effect. To top it off, the quartzite floors were pristine, and the chandeliers were the biggest she'd ever seen. *I gotta call Kent,* Megan thought, *he'd wanna see this.*

Megan quickly slid off to a corner where it was a little quieter to Facetime Kent. He picked up almost right away.

"Hey, you," she said, smiling from ear to ear upon seeing her brother's face.

"What's up, Sis? How's everything going?"

"We're just getting started actually. It's so beautiful in here. Look." Megan turned her phone around so that the camera faced the ballroom. She slowly moved it along so that Kent could see what he was missing.

Kent moved his phone closer to his face. "That's dope, Sis."

104

Megan turned the phone back around to face her. "Isn't it? I wish you were here."

"Me too, but I know you're gonna kill it," Kent said, then flashed her a proud smile.

"Thanks, bro. You just focus on getting better. I'll be up there to see you tomorrow.

"I look forward to it."
Megan ended the Facetime with her brother and rejoined the affair.

A few hours passed by and the night turned out to be a huge success. Megan's art was auctioned off beyond the appraised amounts, and Mark and Laney's idea to display the other four paintings was a hit as well. All fifteen paintings were auctioned off that night. Megan was ecstatic and nothing could ruin her mood. Not even Liam and his date, which she ignored most the night.

As the night was coming to an end, Megan and Laney made their rounds to thank everyone for coming, especially the heavy hitters.

Megan made her way over to a tall and slender Caucasian man who stood admiring a nearby sculpture. The man was well into his 70's but sported a slicked-back, sandy brown, short ponytail with no hint of gray.

Megan noticed earlier that he had spent the most money on one of her paintings.

"Hello Sir, I'm-

"Megan Stone," the man said, gently interrupting her. "There's no need for an introduction."

Megan smiled meekly. "Thank you, Sir. I just wanted to let you know that I appreciate your generous contribution."

"Oh, it wasn't a contribution. I saw something I liked, and I bought it." His stern demeanor caused Megan to chuckle nervously.

"I'm just pulling your leg, dear," he said smiling. "I'm Edward Sanders of the Sanders Gallery in Los Angeles." He held his hand out for Megan to shake.

"That's incredible. I love that place!" Megan said, shaking his hand. She could hardly contain her excitement.

"I'm glad you know of us. And now that we know of you, I'd like to offer you an ongoing contract with my gallery."

Megan's eyes widened. "Oh my- - That's great! Thanks so much." She was almost speechless.

"Have you talked to Dave Gallows? He's co-owner here at Gashange's and a great contact to have in this business if you're going to stay ahead."

"Uh, no. I've never met him." Megan scanned the room as if she'd know who to look for.

"He's the guy in the all gray suit with the blonde hair." Edward pointed to the middle-aged blonde man Megan saw Laney talking to when the event first started.

"Thank you. I'll go and officially introduce myself," Megan said.

"Yes, and I'll be in touch with the negotiations for that contract," he smiled.

"I look forward to it." Megan walked off and headed toward Dave Gallows. However, as she made her way over to him, he started leaving the ballroom. *Oh no,* she thought, *I have to catch him before he leaves.*

She hurried through the crowds of guests and exited the ballroom. Although Megan was a good distance behind him, she managed to follow Dave down a short hallway and then a long one. Before she knew it, she had followed him into an area that appeared to be a loading dock. But just like that, Dave seemed to have disappeared somewhere on the docks.

Megan did an about-face and begin heading back toward the ballroom but was stopped in her tracks when she suddenly heard voices. Against her better judgment, she turned back around and walked toward them. As she got closer, through a cracked door she got a glimpse of four men unloading boxes from a van. Suddenly, Dave appeared to the men and opened one of the boxes with a box cutter. As Megan quietly looked on, Dave pulled out a painting from the box, turned it over and cut a small slit in the back of it. He carefully dug into the slit and pulled out an object that looked to be two sizes larger than a microchip from where Megan stood. Dave looked pleased, and carefully placed the object into a small protective case, then put it into his pocket. Megan was startled when Dave turned and looked to be heading in her direction. She quickly took off her heels and tiptoed out of there as fast as she could.

When Megan made it back to a short hallway entrance that led to the front of the gallery, she assumed she was safe from Dave or anyone else she saw on the loading docks. She breathed a sigh of relief, but it was short-lived when she felt a sudden tap on her shoulder.

Alarmed, Megan gasped and placed her hand over her chest. She almost didn't want to turn around but did anyway. A contrast of relief and annoyance came over her when she saw that it was Liam.

"What are you doing out here? You scared me, idiot." Megan was far from reluctant in letting Liam know she was frustrated with him at that moment.

Unfazed by her unpleasantry, Liam laughed in amusement. "I was looking for the bathroom."

"What's wrong with the ones inside the great ballroom?"

Liam hesitated. "Okay, fine. I saw you leave the ballroom and came looking for you when you took a while to return," he admitted.

"Oh, really? So, your date was okay with you rushing off to look for another woman?" Megan was every bit of sarcastic.

Liam sighed gently. "Megan, come on. Don't be like that. Shayla's a nice girl."

Megan crossed her arms and rolled her eyes. She was annoyed with Liam the second he brought his Cook to her event.

"I knew something was going on between you two."

"No, there wasn't. When you came to my house for dinner, she was just my Cook, seriously."

"I guess she's just irresistible, huh?"

Liam tried to hide his grin but couldn't help it.

"Oh, you think that's funny, huh?" Megan wanted to slap him.

"No...I... Meg, just tell me what's *really* going on. What's wrong?" Liam was finally serious. He knew Megan's attitude had a deeper meaning. Fortunately for him, Megan was in no mood to beat around the bush.

"Liam, I know you gotta have a life. I do, but I just don't think I can deal with you dating anyone right now." Megan had finally calmed down. She wanted Liam to know that she was coming to him from a sincere place and not a jealous one.

Liam nodded. "Are you concerned that I won't be there for you?"

"Yes, I am. It's exactly what I'm afraid of. Right now, I need all of you, Liam." Megan's eyes were fearful.

"You'll always have all of me, Meg." Liam's tone was assuring but Megan could tell that he didn't quite understand.

"Liam, seeing this therapist is unveiling a lot of things for me and making me relive a whole lot of pain. It's also taking me on this journey that I never thought I'd be strong enough to travel. So, no, Liam, I can't have anything or anyone distracting you from being my friend. I'm sorry for how selfish that sounds but it is what it is."

Liam gathered his thoughts for a moment. "I hear you loud and clear, and I promise you that Shayla, is just me having a little fun. She will not get in the way of our friendship."

Megan shook her index finger at him and with all seriousness, she said: "okay, I'm gonna hold you to that promise, Liam."

Chapter 12

Megan found herself back at Dr. Green's office just two days after the Gashange's event. She was elated by the turnout and the potential clients the event brought her. However, she wasn't there to talk about her work as much as she needed to fill Dr. Green in on the meeting with her Uncle Stan.

"So how did that meeting make you feel?" Dr. Green asked. She was sitting in her chair and this time she had a pen and pad resting in her lap. Megan took notice and wondered what this change was all about.

"Are you not recording today?" she asked instead of answering Dr. Green's question.

Dr. Green looked down at her pen and pad. "Oh, this is for our next exercise. I'll tell you more about it when it's time, okay?" Dr. Green smiled a warm smile. Megan returned the smile but remained silent.

"Still having a hard time trusting the process I see."

Megan nodded. "I guess. Sorry."

"It's okay. It's totally normal. And to answer your question; yes, we are recording this session. That will never change, and if for some reason it does, I will let you know."

"Thanks," Megan said looking down at her nails. Dr. Green sat back in her chair and folded her hands. It was a neat little trick she did that always got Megan to fill in the awkward silence. Dr. Green wasn't afraid of silence, but Megan was. All Dr. Green had to do when Megan played hardball was sit back and shut up. Eventually, Megan would become so uncomfortable, she'd spill all the beans. The trick never failed and before long, Megan filled Dr. Green in on everything that happened from the meeting with Stan to everything that took place at Gashange's. This included her following Dave Gallows to the loading dock and her hallway conversation with Liam.

"A lot has happened since we last met. Let's start with the meeting with Stan. How did it make you feel afterward?"

"I walked away feeling bad for how I've treated him. But I also walked away feeling like I still have more questions about my father's disappearance."

"Is this due to the allegations he made about your father's bank accounts?"

Megan sighed. "Yes."

Dr. Green could see Megan's level of discomfort beginning to rise. "I know this is hard for you, Megan." She paused then said: "let's talk about Liam."

"Okay, what about him?" Megan was happy to change the subject.

"I know he's your friend, but do you think you have deeper feelings for him?"

"No, of course not." Megan shifted in her seat. Dr. Green could see that this question also made Megan uncomfortable, but it was a discomfort she knew Megan could handle.

"It's okay if you do, Meg. He seems like a great guy."

"He *is* a great guy. Which is why we can never date. I'd hate to lose him as my friend."

"I understand," Dr. Green said in her calm voice. "So, what do you think about Shayla?"

"I don't know what to think of her. I don't wanna worry about her because I'm worried about me."

"Hmm," Dr. Green said curiously. She lightly tapped her pen against the palm of her hand as she appeared to be in deep thought. She flashed Megan an understanding smile and nod, then continued. "The conversation you had with Liam; it makes sense. This journey is a scary one for you. So, I can see why you would ask such a thing of your friend."

"Do you think I was wrong?" Megan asked, worriedly.

"I'm not here to tell you whether you're wrong or right, Meg. But I will tell you that this process has the potential to get lonely for you, no matter how many people you have in your corner."

Megan swallowed hard. "Well, I wanna prevent that as much as possible."

"As long as you trust the process completely, we can do that together. The loneliness comes when you put up the walls."

Megan nodded. Dr. Green then picked up her pen and wrote something on the pad. "We've come to a place in your therapy where I will start writing you prescriptions." She tore the top sheet off the pad and handed it to Megan.

"So that was a prescription pad you had the whole time?" Megan said, taking the script and reading it. "Cooking class?"

"Yes. The prescriptions I write for you will be external exercises that will help you on the path to healing."

"What does attending a cooking class have to do with anything?" Megan said. She was confused, to say the least.

"As usual, while listening to our recorded sessions I am able to go in-depth with the things you have revealed to me. I have come to notice that you loved your father's cooking. In your last conversation with him, he tried to tell you the secret to how he made his pancakes just the way you liked them, correct?"

"Yes, that's correct," Megan said softly.

"And, these recordings have revealed to me that you don't cook, right?"

Megan nodded.

"Megan, that last conversation with your father has created a negative connotation in your mind when it comes to cooking. It appears you associate cooking with loss. This could be the reason you are not too fond of Shayla. She's a Cook whom you think is here to take your friend away."

"No, that doesn't make any sense," Megan snapped in denial.

"Okay, then how about you take the cooking class to help you reconnect with your father in memory. You could keep his memory alive just by doing something that he loved to do. Even if he can't be there to enjoy it with you."

Megan thought for a moment. "Can I invite others to come with me?"

"Absolutely. It would be a perfect opportunity to create new memories as well."

"Okay, I'll do it."

"Good," Dr. Green said, relieved. "All you have to do is call the number and set it up."

Megan quickly changed the subject. "Hey, what do you think about what I saw at Gashange's? On the loading docks?"

"I think the activity sounds a bit strange. More reason for you not to worry yourself about it since you already have enough on your plate, correct?"

"True." Megan agreed with Dr. Green but hearing her say that the activity seemed strange only made Megan more suspicious. *What was going on at Gashange's?* she thought.

Chapter 13

Megan let herself into her mother's house. She walked down the wide hall and into the kitchen. "Mom, I'm here. Where are you guys," she called out while placing her keys on one of the counters.

"In here," Keres called from the dining room. Megan walked into the dining room and was overjoyed to see her brother sitting at the table. She ran over, bent down and gave him a tight squeeze. "I'm sorry I couldn't be there when you were discharged."

"It's cool, Sis. I know you have things to do. But look what I got you." Kent lifted a wrapped gift that rested on the side of his chair and gave it to Megan.

"What?... When did you have time to get me something? And what's the occasion?" Megan was beaming with excitement.

"I ordered it. I wanted to get you something since I wasn't there for your event. Plus, it's a token of appreciation for saving my life."

Megan had tears in her eyes before she even knew what Kent got her. The gesture alone was sweet and heartfelt, and she didn't care what it was. She tore off the wrapping paper and unveiled a beautiful painting. She examined the painting and realized it was a piece by Enri de Fere, a famous French painter.

"This is awesome! How did you get your hands on this?" Megan said and kissed Kent's forehead.

"I called in a favor to your girl Laney and she came through. That girl is a beast when it comes to getting things done."

"Don't I know it. But how did Laney get her hands on an Enri de Fere? These are a rarity. I've wanted one forever." Megan was grateful but her curiosity was piqued to the max.

"She said she cut some type of deal with one of the partners at Gashange's. I gave her the money, along with her cut, and she took care of the rest."

"Oh, she over here making side money?" Megan laughed.

"It was just this once," Kent chuckled.

That's why I saw her talking to Dave at the start of the event, Megan thought, connecting the dots. *But what kind of deal did she make?* she wondered.

"Are you two done now? I'd like to eat dinner. It's bad enough you're late," Keres said irritated.

"Nice to see you too, mother."

Keres ignored Megan's comment and called for Henrietta the maid to serve their dinner.

Noticing Keres' attitude, Megan realized that she was the one who didn't greet her mother when she came in.

"I'm sorry, mom. I was just excited to see Kent. How are you today? Megan said as she went to hug her mother.

Keres cracked a smile and returned Megan's embrace. "It's okay, and I'm doing fine. Just have a seat so we can get this dinner started."

Megan did as she was told and sat down at the table.

Moments later, Henrietta brought out dinner for everyone, and the family peacefully ate without saying much at all. But, after becoming tired of the silence, Megan spoke up.

"So, mom, I missed you at my event."

"Sweetie, you know I never go to those functions."

"I know, but it would be nice if you would."

"Honey, I've already explained this. It's nothing personal. I just want your events to be about you and *only* you. My presence would only ruin that."

120

Although Keres' statement was seemingly arrogant, there was some truth to it. She had made a name for herself over the years and became quite the socialite. Each marriage brought her more popularity as her newest husband was always richer than the last.

"If you say so, mom." Megan already knew what her mother's answer would be, but she wanted Keres to know that her absence bothered her. Dealing with her emotions was something she was learning to do in therapy, but she was afraid that it would never work on her mother.

"I'm sorry I wasn't there, Meg. But it was for your own good," Keres said trying to help Megan understand.

Megan feigned a smile, but what she really wanted to do was roll her eyes. Yet, no matter how ridiculous her mother sounded, she would not disrespect her.

"I'm just glad everything turned out well for you, Sis. I knew you were gonna kill it," Kent said to ease the tension. Megan gave Kent a knowing smile, then decided to change the subject.

"I met with Uncle Stan the other day, Kent."

Keres raised a brow. "Why would you do that?" she asked.

"Why shouldn't I have? Kent convinced me that I shouldn't be angry with him."

"That's good, Meg," Kent chimed in. "I'm proud of you."

Keres shot him a venomous look. Noticing, Megan looked at her mother with furrowed brows. She couldn't understand why it was such a big deal meeting with Uncle Stan, and her mother's sudden anger was surprising to her.

"Mom, I thought you and Uncle Stan left off on good terms?" Megan asked.

"We did," Keres said sharply.

"Whoa, mom. Chill out," Kent added. Keres just cut her eyes at him.

Ignoring her mother's unpleasantness, Megan pressed on. "So why do you seem upset that I met with him?"

"Because we need to leave the past in the past. We've been over this," Keres said flustered.

Megan sighed, while Kent looked on in confusion.

"Uncle Stan is *your* past, mom, not mine," he declared. "You've always known that I had a relationship with him, so what's the problem now?"

"The problem is that your relationship with Stan is genuine. Your sister, however, only wants to reconnect so she could stir some stuff up about your father."

"And that's a bad thing *because?*" Kent needed clarity on his mother's statement. There was silence in the dining room for a moment as Kent and Megan waited for their mother's response.

"You wouldn't understand, son," Keres said defeated.

Kent could see that his mother was uncomfortable and decided to leave it alone, but Megan had other plans. "The truth is that Mom has thrown our dad away, along with anyone else attached to him, because she doesn't want to deal with her emotions."

"That is not true," Keres retorted.

"Really? Then why don't you ever talk about him? Why haven't you spoken to our grandmother in over a decade."

"She lives in Sri Lanka!"

"That can't be your excuse, mom," Kent said. He was calm but his tone let Keres know that her answer was unacceptable.

Megan scoffed and stood up from the table.

"I'm not staying here for this nonsense, Kent. If you want to accept that mom never wants to talk about dad, then you do that. I'm done." Megan went into the kitchen to grab her keys off the counter, then walked through the foyer and out the front door. She was fuming beyond measure.

Meanwhile back at the dining room table, Keres buried her face in her hands and Kent was speechless. Still, there were things he wanted to say. He wanted to call Megan back but knew she needed her space. He wanted to ask his mother why she always ran from any conversation regarding his father, but he left that alone too.

Later that night, Megan lay awake in her bed all night staring at the ceiling. There was no way she could sleep while she thought about her mother's heated disapproval of meeting with Stan. Megan couldn't understand Keres' reasoning and it only made her think that her mother had something to hide. The thought also caused her to revisit the initial idea that Kent's paternity was questionable. *Maybe Uncle Stan was lying to me,* she thought, *or maybe he wasn't and someone else is Kent's father.* Whatever her thoughts, Megan's suspicions were back in full force and would not leave her this time.

Megan quickly got out of bed and went over to her walk-in closet. She turned on the light and pulled a keepsake box from the shelf. She opened it and retrieved what she was looking for. It was the picture of her family that her dog Cooper almost tore apart a few weeks ago. She examined the picture. This time she looked more at her father's face and then her brother's. She was disappointed that she saw no resemblance. All she saw when she looked at Kent's face in the picture was her mother. A wave of sadness came over her. Although this was not proof enough to question her brother's paternity, she couldn't help to think now more than ever that there was a secret behind who fathered her brother. *I must get to the bottom of this,* she thought.

Chapter 14

The next day Megan reluctantly pulled into her mother's driveway. She gathered her thoughts for a moment before she got out of the car. Earlier this morning after Megan woke up, she immediately called Laney; groggy voice and all, to tell her that she wouldn't be in the office until much later.

She finally got out of the car, walked up to the front door and used her key to let herself in. "Mom!" she called out but there was no answer. Megan scanned the first floor for her mother. "Mom?" she called again. Still no answer. Megan made her way upstairs and down the corridor that would eventually lead to her mother's master bedroom. She called for her mother again, "mom." But this time it was Kent who poked his head out of his bedroom, startling her.

"Hey Sis, I didn't expect you to be back so soon."

"Neither did I, but I came to apologize to mom," Megan lied.

"That's cool, but she ain't here."

"What about her husband? He here?"

"Nope." Kent leaned his back against the wall.

"Okay, then I guess I'll just hang out in my old room for a little while."

"Cool. I would hang with you, but I just took these painkillers for my leg. I'm 'bout to be knocked out soon."

Okay, bro. Just focus on getting better," Megan said, masking her relief. She kissed his cheek and walked toward her old bedroom. When she arrived at the door, she looked to her left to see if Kent was still watching. Thankfully, he wasn't, and she could see that his bedroom door was now closed. In the clear, Megan headed further down the hallway and into her mother's bedroom.

As Megan entered her mother's room, she saw that everything was neat and well organized just as it had been during her childhood. Megan knew her mother's house like the back of her hand. It was the house they had moved into after she married her Uncle Stan. Megan was happy at this moment that no matter how many times her mother got remarried, she never moved. It made Megan's task of finding what she was looking for a lot easier. Only, she didn't know what she was looking for.

Megan went straight to her mother's walk-in closet which was the size of her childhood bedroom just down the hall, also considerably large. She grabbed the first storage bin she saw, took the lid off and began carefully looking through it. She didn't want her mother to notice that her things had been messed with.

Megan went through each bin, regardless of its labeling, but still found nothing of worth. Frustrated, she desperately scanned the closet hoping that something of significance would appear, but there was nothing. Still, Megan was determined not to give up. She exited the closet and walked toward her mother's desk which was on the far side of her apartment-sized bedroom. As she walked, she appreciated the feel of her mother's soft white plush carpet brushing between her toes.

She arrived at the desk which had three drawers on the left and a middle pull-out drawer. Megan started with the pull-out drawer which to no surprise was locked. Being prepared, Megan reached into her purse and pulled out two bobby pins; one to serve as the lock pick and the other to serve as the tension wrench. Thanks to Kent, she learned to pick her mother's locks all the time growing up.

Before attempting to pick the lock, she tiptoed to the bedroom door and looked down the hall to make sure the coast was still clear with Kent. She also paused a moment to ensure that she didn't hear any other signs of life in the house. When all was clear, she tiptoed back to the desk and proceeded to pick the lock. First, she inserted the bobby pin that substituted a tension wrench to apply gentle pressure inside the keyhole, then she inserted the bobby pin that substituted a lock pick. After a few twists and jiggles, the lock opened, and she happily pulled the drawer open. As she looked through the drawer, she could see that there were documents that seemed to be important. However, the one thing that stood out to her was a large manila envelope. The envelope was thick, which led Megan to believe there had to be a lot of items stuffed inside. She picked up the large envelope, unfastened the string that held it closed and opened it. The first thing she noticed was a blue folder, so she pulled the folder out of the large envelope, then opened that too. Maintaining her carefulness, Megan slowly went through the materials in the folder and stopped when she came across a small unsealed envelope with the words "Mom's keys" on it. With furrowed brows, Megan opened it. In the envelope, there were two keys on a key ring, and on the ring; a white tag with six numbers on it. Megan had no clue what she was looking at, but she was sure going to find out. She skimmed through the documents in the folder and finally found something that started to make sense. It was a document describing her maternal grandmother's burial plan. She skimmed through the rest of the documents and saw that the whole folder was dedicated to the plan. She found another document that had a set of serial numbers on it. She looked at the six numbers on the key tag, and they matched. *Are these keys for the mausoleum?* she thought. *Why would she have a key? And why would there be two?* Megan couldn't understand the purpose of the keys, but she knew who to ask. She tucked the keys in her pocket, placed everything back the way it was and left the house.

Chapter 15

Megan walked down the hall to Liam's office after his receptionist gave her entry past the front desk. When she left her mother's house, she stopped at a hardware store to have copies of the keys made, went back to her mother's house, and put the original keys back where she found them. She closed and locked the drawer and made it so no one knew she was ever there. All the while, Kent was still asleep and thankfully her mother wasn't home. Now she was at Liam's office, the one person she hoped could answer her questions about the keys.

"Knock, knock," Megan said sticking her head into Liam's office.

"Hey, come on in," Liam smiled. He stood up from his seat to hug Megan. They embraced, then Liam went back to sit at his desk while Megan remained standing.

"I don't mean to bombard you or anything, but I came to ask you something, and then I'm gone because I have to get back to work myself."

"Okay, it's no problem, Meg. What's up?"

"I found these keys at my mother's house." Megan handed the keys to Liam. "The documents said they're to my grandmother's mausoleum?"

Liam gave Megan a concerning look. "What do you mean you *found* these at your mother's house? You been snooping around over there or something?"

Megan huffed. "Not right now, Liam. I don't need questions, I need answers. Please, tell me why someone would need keys to a mausoleum?"

"Why should I know?" Liam said confused.

"Are you kidding me? You worked at a cemetery while you were in Med School. Or did you forget?"

"Ahh," Liam said clasping his hands. "I almost *did* forget. This med stuff takes over my mind sometimes," he joked.

"Well, I know you gotta get back to work, so tell me what they're for."

"I'd love to know why you have them in the first place," Liam said eyeing her suspiciously.

"Liam?!" she wined.

He sighed deeply, then paused, then sighed again. Megan could see that she was causing Liam, a normally easygoing guy, to be distressed.

"I promise I'll tell you when the time comes," she said sincerely. "I just need to sort some things out first."

Liam nodded feebly then proceeded with his answer. "Sometimes people... mostly wealthy, have keys to a single crypt mausoleum. These people pay loads of money to have a private sanctuary that holds the crypt. It's not a large building, but it's a big enough space that could be compared to a small chapel. The ones I saw even had a pew or two, and air conditioning. They're nice. If your grandmother is resting in one of these, your mother is richer than I thought," he said, handing her back the keys.

"Yeah well, my grandmother died a few months before I was born, so it was my father's money that paid for it."

"Hmph, then Megha was *mega*-rich," Liam said returning to his lighthearted self.

"Very funny," Megan smirked. "Anyway, I get the one key, but why two?"

Liam shrugged. "You got me there. Maybe she has two locks on it."

"Hmm, maybe. I'm not sure why it matters so much to me, but I just feel weird about these keys, Liam."

"Weird how?"

"I don't know. I'll admit that I was snooping but I wasn't expecting to find these keys and feel so drawn to them. I'm almost...scared."

Liam frowned. He was becoming more concerned about her. He didn't understand what she was up to. However, she already told him that she would explain later so he left it alone, even though he didn't want to. "Just be careful, Megan. Whatever you're doing, all I ask is that you be careful."

"I will," she said flashing a warm smile.

Liam nodded. Megan could see the concern on his face. "I'll be alright. I'm not doing anything crazy," she attempted to assure him.

"I know," was all he managed to say. Liam wasn't concerned about her doing anything crazy. He was concerned about her mental health. He never liked it when Megan obsessed over things because she'd often end up depressed and behind on her work. Most of the things she obsessed over weren't worth it and he hoped that wasn't the case this time.

"Well, I gotta get to work, hon. I'll call you later." She blew him a kiss and turned on her heels to exit his office.

"Meg, wait. I just remembered something."

Megan turned to face him. "What's that?"

"When I worked as a grounds crew member, sometimes we'd have these conversations about the rich and their mausoleums."

"Okay, about what?"

"There was this one man who would come visit his loved one all the time, or so we thought. One day he came there with a small bag in his hand. Of course, he didn't think anyone was watching, but *we* were, from afar. Anyway, when he came back out, he didn't have the bag with him anymore. The rest of the crew and I were curious, so later that day we asked our boss about it and he said the strangest thing."

"What, what did he say?"

"He said 'you'd be surprised that some people stash things other than their loved ones' remains in there.' I can't believe I forgot about that. I mean we even talked about how genius it was to put something of value in a crypt. It's the last place in the world anybody would think to look."

Megan just stood there staring into space. She was horrified. If she was on edge before, Liam's story just pushed her over.

"You alright, Meg?"

"Uh, yeah," she exhaled deeply. "That was a strange story."

"Yes, it was, and a true one. As a friend, I tried my best to give you the answers you came here looking for, which to me was also strange."

"And I thank you for that. I do," she said defensively.

"But you don't like my answers, right?"

"I didn't say that," she said shifting uncomfortably. "I just don't know what to think of them."

"How 'bout you don't think of them at all, and just leave the whole thing alone."

"I can't. I told you, there's something weird about these keys. And that story you told just gave me the creeps."

"Well, do what you want. But remember this; curiosity killed the cat, Megan, and you need to sit your curious behind down."

Megan shuddered at his words.

Chapter 16

"Curiosity killed the cat, Megan," was all she kept hearing in her head. Megan finally made it to her office but couldn't get any work done. *Why did he have to say that?* she thought. *Why can't he just be supportive and shut up sometimes?*

"Maybe my curiosity is too much for me," she told herself. She leaned back in her chair in heavy thought. There was no way she was giving up on this. No matter what Liam said. She was determined to get answers, whatever that meant. At this point, Megan didn't even know the type of answers she was looking for anymore. At first, it was the question of Kent's paternity, but finding the keys created a game-changer and she was now aimlessly searching.

Exhausted, she laid her head on her desk. *I'm gonna leave this alone,* she thought, *for now.*

Later that day, Megan stuck to her guns and left the whole "key situation" alone. She decided to finally take Dr. Green's advice and schedule a cooking session. When she called the number Dr. Green gave her, she was able to book a session for tomorrow evening. Megan was thrilled that there was an opening so soon. She invited Kent, Liam, and Laney and they all told her they'd be there. She hoped this session would prove to be as therapeutic as Dr. Green claimed it would be.

After Megan scheduled her cooking session, she also booked an appointment with the private investigator Dr. Green also referred her to. She figured if she was no longer going to stress over the keys to her grandmother's crypt, then at least she could start the investigation on her father's abduction and disappearance.

That night as Megan lay her head down on her pillow, she was relieved that she was able to fall asleep right away. Her body and mind needed the rest, and she was fine with anything that would keep her mind off those keys.

When she arose in the morning, she felt refreshed. She went for her morning run, then returned home to shower and get dressed for work. Today was the day she would create a new memory with the important people in her life. Although Dr. Green was on to something about Megan shying away from cooking due to her past trauma; she wasn't anxious about the cooking class. Megan figured that it was because the class turned out to be a welcomed distraction.

◻◻◻◻◻◻◻◻◻

It was an easy day at the office for Megan and the time seemed to breeze by. She logged off her computer, gathered her things, then called Laney into her office.

"Yes, boss lady?" Laney said as she entered Megan's office.

"I wanted to talk to you before we left for the cooking class."

"Okay, what about?"

"First off, I'd like to thank you for hooking Kent up with that Enri de Fere painting. I love it."

"Oh, so he told you it was me?" Laney responded; a bit surprised.

"Was he not supposed to?"

"Uh, I don't know. I just thought he wanted to keep it a secret."

"Well, he was going to, but you know me. There's no way he's coming to me with a painting like that and I'm not gonna ask any questions."

Laney nodded in agreement.

"Trust me, the gesture was beautiful, and I appreciate it," Megan assured her. "But what's this deal you made with Dave Gallows?"

As Laney stood in the doorway, she nervously slid her hands into her pockets and glanced down at her shoes. Reading Laney's body language, Megan said: "that bad, huh?"

"No. It's just that I'm not sure you'd approve."

"What is it?" Megan asked sternly.

"He asked me if he could store some of his paintings here since the warehouse at Gashange's is getting a bit overcrowded."

"That doesn't sound so bad," Megan said relieved. "How long does he want this to go on?"

"He said it would be just for a few months."

"Fine, but I'm only okay with this because I know you did it to help Kent. But please don't ever make a deal like that again without speaking with me first. We could be charging him a storage fee, girl."

Laney chuckled. "I know. That's why I was nervous to tell you about it."

"It's alright. If that's what it took to get me my de Fere, then so be it," Megan said smiling. "Now let's go. I don't want to be late for this cooking class."

Chapter 17

Megan and Laney arrived together at Mae's Kitchen where Megan signed in and registered her party for the class. A young receptionist escorted Megan and Laney to a large kitchen area in the back of the establishment. It was a basic kitchen with all silver appliances and silver countertops. The atmosphere was neat and clean, and Megan could smell the sweet aroma of food in the air. It was a lingering odor of food cooked in the previous session.

"Welcome ladies." A short plump middle-aged looking woman seemed to suddenly appear in the room. "I'm Mae, the owner of this kitchen, and I'll be your instructor this evening."

"It's a pleasure to meet you, Ms. Mae," Megan said smiling kindly. She could see that the woman looked to be about sixty.

"Yes, thanks for having us," added Laney.

"I was told there was going to be four of you," said Mae. She pulled a small rag from her apron pocket to wipe her face and forehead. Her dark brown skin was smooth but clammy looking, and the sweat seemed to have reappeared just as soon as it was wiped away.

"There are two more coming, ma'am," Megan told her. "They should be here any minute."

"Alright, but if they're not here on time, we will have to start without them." Mae looked down at her watch. "That gives them five more minutes."

"Yes ma'am," Megan said.

Just then, Kent came hobbling in, using his cane for assistance.

"Hey," Megan said. She walked over to Kent and hugged him.

"What's up, Sis... How are you doing, Laney?"

"I'm doing great, even though you snitched on me to your sister."

Kent let out a hearty chuckle. "My bad," was all he could say.

"Whatever," Laney said playfully.

Megan laughed in amusement at her brother and Laney's exchange.

"Hello, my good people!" Liam said. He stood in the entryway of the kitchen with his hands on his hips, imitating Superman.

Megan giggled softly. Her spirits were lifted and the last few moments made her forget about all her troubles.

"Would you stop playing and come on so we can get this session started," Megan said, maintaining her smile.

Liam greeted them all one by one, then they all took a seat at their stations. Liam sat next to Megan, and Kent sat next to Laney. "Today you will be learning how to make spaghetti and meatballs," announced Mae. "It's a simple meal but this is a beginner's class. When you're ready to really get down in the kitchen, you can come back and attend one of my soul food sessions."
The crew nodded simultaneously, and Liam gave Megan a thumbs up.

"This was a great idea, Meg," he whispered.

"Thanks," she whispered back.

"Hi everyone. Got room for one more?"

Megan was suddenly thrown off by the sound of an unfamiliar female voice. She most certainly wasn't expecting anyone else to show up since everyone she invited was already there.

Her whole mood changed when she saw none other than Shayla standing in the kitchen doorway. Megan instantly shot Liam a disapproving look. "What the hell is she doing here, Liam?"

"I'm sorry, Meg. We had a date tonight and I didn't wanna cancel."

"So, you bring her here? On my time?" Megan couldn't believe the nerve on Liam. "I thought we discussed this?"

"I know, but I didn't want her to think I was blowing her off for you. I don't want her to think we have something going on, you know?"

Megan laughed incredulously. "You are unbelievable."

"What?" Liam said dumbfounded. Before Megan could respond, Shayla was standing in front of them.

"Is it okay if I sit here?" Shayla said referring to the empty space between them.

"There's no stool there," Megan responded snidely.

"That's no problem. I'll just pull one up," Shayla said. Just like that, Shayla took a spare stool and placed it right between Megan and Liam. Now she was the one sitting next to him. Megan tried her best to maintain her composure. Her mood was completely ruined and at this point, she wanted nothing more than to just go home. Kent and Laney looked on curiously but didn't say a word. However, they both realized that Megan no longer seemed to be cheerful.

"Okay, everybody please go over the list of ingredients in front of you, and make sure you have everything on that list," Mae said moving on with the lesson.

The crew did what they were told, and before anyone knew it, a half-hour had passed by. Megan barely said a word the whole time, except for a nod here and there, and a few short word exchanges with Laney and Kent. Liam and Shayla, on the other hand, seemed to be having the most fun. The flirtatious giggling was enough to make Megan go mad, but she pressed on remembering that she was there to honor her father's memory.

"Uh, Ms. Mae, I'm having a little trouble here. Does my meat look done to you?" Megan asked.

"Let's see," Mae said as she examined Megan's meat with a wooden spoon. "Almost, just let it cook a little longer. You want it to brown. That's how you'll know it's done."

"Thanks," Megan said.

Shayla burst out laughing. "You mean to tell me you don't know how to cook ground meat?"

Megan gave Liam a disgusted look before responding to Shayla. "Since you must know, I don't know how to cook. Period."

"Hmph, some wife you'll make," Shayla mocked.

"Are you gonna just sit there while she disrespects me like this?" Megan asked Liam.

"I...uh...can you both just please stop?" Liam managed to say.

"Both of us?" Megan asked bewildered. "She started it. Not to mention, none of this would be happening if you didn't bring her here in the first place!"

"I'm here because Liam wants me here," Shayla chimed in.

"Okay, that's enough ladies," Mae said trying to bring order back to her class.

"Who cares what Liam wants. This is my event," Megan said sharply. "Besides, you're a chef. Why would you want to be here anyway?" Megan was fuming at this point and she hardly recognized that she ignored poor Ms. Mae's instruction.

"Sis, just chill," Kent said. He was tired of sitting quietly while Shayla disrespected his sister. "We're here for dad. Don't let her ruin that. She's not worth it."

"Well, Liam seems to think I'm worth it," said Shayla. "And I'm not doing anything wrong by being here."

"You really believe that, huh?" Megan said.

"Yes, I do," Shayla responded righteously. "Everyone knows that you're just on edge all the time because of what happened to your father when you were little."

"Excuse me?" Megan said in disbelief. She looked to Liam who now had his face buried in his hands.

"You heard what I said. All you do is cry victim all day long, running to Liam with all your problems. Well, that act is over now, honey. So, you can go somewhere else with your daddy issues, okay?"

"Shay!" Liam finally spoke up. Only it was too late. Before anybody knew it, Megan swung and punched Shayla right out of her stool.

"Megan?! Are you kidding me?" Liam shouted as he quickly kneeled to help Shayla up from the floor.

"Are you seriously asking me that right now?" Megan felt betrayed.

"It's time for you all to leave this place, now!" Mae shouted. Laney gently grabbed Megan by the arm and pulled her back from Shayla. Kent stood from his stool and limped toward the door. "Come on, Sis. Let's go before they call the cops or something."

"I am definitely pressing charges," Shayla spat with her hand covering her right eye. "You are a classless heathen, Megan. I can't believe Liam associates himself with such filth."

Megan ignored Shayla's rant. Instead, she gave Liam a hateful glare. "I don't ever want to speak to you again," she told him, then stormed out of the kitchen with Kent and Laney in tow.

"Meg, wait, please," Liam called after her, but his plea fell on deaf ears. He turned to Shayla and gave a puzzled look.

"Why would you do that?" he asked her.

"Do what? She needed to know that you can no longer be her crutch."

Liam scoffed. "She is my friend, Shay."

"*Was* your friend. She wants nothing to do with you now. Looks like I won, but I'm still pressing charges," Shayla said smirking.

Liam was too angry to respond. He stormed out of the kitchen, leaving Shayla there with her jaw dropped.

Chapter 18

Liam dashed out of Mae's Kitchen and straight into the parking lot. He spotted Megan and Laney who were watching as Kent got into his car and drove away.

"Megan, wait up!" Liam called. Megan looked back at Liam and quickly got into her car. Laney followed suit, and Megan backed out of the parking space like a madwoman. She sped right by Liam, who wasn't going to give up that easily. He ran to his car, jumped in and sped off right behind her. As Megan was stopped at a red light, Liam pulled up beside her to get her attention. Only that didn't work, and Megan ran the light just to get away from him. Against his better judgment, Liam ran the light as well and sped up behind her. He beeped the horn like a maniac as Megan weaved in and out of traffic. After chasing her for about half a mile, Megan finally pulled her car into a vacant parking lot. Liam pulled in behind her, quickly parked his car, and got out. Megan was already standing outside of her car with her arms folded.

"Have you lost your mind?" she said irately. You could've caused an accident."

"Please, just hear me out."

"There's nothing to talk about. You betrayed me." Megan's voice was angry, but her eyes were sad.

"I'm so sorry, Megan. I should've never brought her there."

"That's beside the point now. You've been telling her things about me, about my life, and what happened to my father."

"It wasn't like that, I promise."

"Then what was it like, Liam? Tell me," Megan demanded.

"I tried to explain to her that we needed to take it slow because you've been through a lot."

"Let me guess, this is after you promised me that she wouldn't get in between our friendship?"

"Yes, but-

"I don't know what that promise meant to you," Megan interjected, "but to me, it meant that you weren't supposed to see her again."

"Megan, please. I'm sorry."

"You went behind my back! Did you want to be with her that bad?"

"No, I just-

"And then you flaunted her in my face. At this point, I don't know if you were being disrespectful or just plain stupid."

"If you would let me talk, I could explain. Please." Liam was calm, but still a little worried that Megan wouldn't forgive him.

"Make it quick then," Megan said sharply.

"I was wrong to bring her, especially without asking you, and especially after I promised you I wouldn't see her anymore. But Megan, I'm only getting older and I wanna find someone I can settle down with. You want me to wait until you find the closure you need, and I understand that. But I would be lying if I told you I could hold off on dating just so I could be an available friend to you."

"But why is that so bad?" Megan asked. "I know it was a lot to ask but it's what I need." Tears streamed down her face.

"It may be what you need, Meg, but I can't stop my life for you," Liam said gently.

"So, what are you saying?"

"I'm saying it's not a fair thing to ask."

"Then why didn't you just tell me that instead of making a false promise?" Megan was still irritated, but less angry now.

"At the time I thought I could keep my promise, but then I got lonely."

There was a brief silence between them. Before continuing their conversation, Megan looked into her car to see what Laney was doing. She was relieved to see that Laney was on the phone engaging in her own conversation.

"How could I ever forgive you?" Megan proceeded. "You told a stranger my business and now thanks to you, she thinks I'm a miserable, clingy, little fool."

"I promise you, all I told her was that your father disappeared when you were younger, and you've been through a lot because of it. I told her that she and I needed to take things slow because you needed me now more than ever. She's the one who added all that other stuff."

"So, I should forgive you because she twisted your words?"

"I would hope so. I don't take anything you've been through lightly. You should know this by now."

"I don't know what I know anymore."

Liam sighed. "I'm sorry. I just failed at trying to juggle both of you. I thought I could."

"If she were a different kind of woman, you might've succeeded."

Before Liam could answer, Kent pulled up. "Hey guys, sorry to interrupt but Laney called me to come pick her up," Kent informed them.

Just then, Laney climbed out of Megan's car and walked over to Kent's.

"Oh, Laney, I'm so sorry, hon."

"It's fine, Meg. I just wanted to give you guys your space to hash things out."

"Are you sure?" Megan asked concerned.

"I'm positive. You two finish talking," said Laney as she climbed into Kent's Range Rover. Megan thanked Laney and Kent, then watched as they drove off.

Megan sighed. "I need to get home myself, Liam."

"Yeah, I know," Liam said feeling defeated. Megan turned to walk toward her car.

"Meg, you know I love you."

"Yes, I know," she said softly.

"Do you?" Liam asked seriously.

Megan raised a brow. "What?"

"I've loved you all these years as far as you'd let me. It's time you let me love you, the way a man truly loves a woman."

"Where is this coming from, Liam?"

"Years of restraint, that's where. Do you think it was fun for me to see you date other men and pretend I was unfazed?"

Megan sighed deeply. "Liam, we can't."

"And why not?" he said gently grabbing her arms and pulling her close to him. "I know you love me too. So why not?"

As he looked into Megan's eyes, her heart melted as it normally did. This time she didn't look away.

"I could be your friend and your lover too."

"You can't," she whispered.

"I can," he said softly, and gently kissed her lips. Unable to resist, Megan found herself returning Liam's advances and they shared a long and passionate kiss.

When they finally came up for air, Megan looked into Liam's eyes and said: "what about Shayla?"

"What about her?" Liam replied nonchalantly.

"If we're gonna give us a shot, you'll have to cut her loose."

"Absolutely. That goes without saying."

Megan smiled. *Could this be happening?* she thought, *will this actually work?* For all her thoughts she certainly hoped so. Liam declaring his love for her was unexpected, but she welcomed it. She was still afraid, but Liam was easy to love, and the point he

155

made about being lovers and friends suddenly made sense to her.

"So, you'd give up Shayla, for me?" Megan asked.

"Of course. Compared to what you and I have, Shayla means nothing. When you told me you never wanted to speak to me again, I couldn't stand the thought of it. As far as I'm concerned, I already made my choice when I came chasing after you."

"But Shayla doesn't seem like the kind of woman that would just give up so easily," Megan said concerned.

"That doesn't matter. She won't be getting any of my time, trust me."

"But she knows where you live and everything. Hopefully, she doesn't stalk you," Megan said half-jokingly.

Liam chuckled. "She'd have to get past my building's security guard first."

"I don't know. This just makes things worse, especially since she said she's pressing charges."

"Don't worry. I know how to handle Shayla. I gotchu, babe. Don't you know I'd do anything for you, Meg? Anything."

Chapter 19

The next day at the office Megan had a hard time concentrating on her work. The incident with Shayla flooded her mind. The last thing she needed was a lawsuit or criminal charges being filed against her. "I can't believe I let her bring me out of character like that," she said to herself.

Megan was embarrassed by her behavior. In a sense she believed Shayla was right about one thing; she was classless for socking her. Yet, at the time it felt like sweet justice. But truth be told, punching Shayla wasn't totally out of character for Megan. During Megan's freshman year in high school, she had gone through an angry phase in which she threw fits and became physically aggressive toward other students. However, Liam and Laney had never seen that side of Megan. As far as they were concerned, she *was* full of class and a very levelheaded businesswoman. Besides, those days were long behind her now and she wanted to kick herself for getting out of pocket.

Just then Laney peeked her head in the doorway of Megan's office.

"Hey, boss lady. Your mom is on Line 1."

"Oh no," Megan groaned. "Did she say what she wanted?"

"Nope, just said she needed me to put her through."

"Okay, thanks. I got it from here."

Laney went about her business, while Megan picked up the phone and pressed Line 1. "Hi mom," Megan said dryly. She knew exactly what this call was about. Her mother had been blowing up her cell phone all morning, and Megan knew it was just a matter of time before Keres would call the office.

"Megan, what were you thinking? I can't believe you hit someone!" her mother shouted from the other end.

Of course, Kent had to go running his mouth, she thought. *Mama's boy.*

"Mom, I know, okay? Please don't rub it in. I already can't stop thinking about it."

"Well, you're going to be thinking about it a heck of a lot more if she goes through with pressing charges."

"I know. Let's just hope it doesn't come to that," Megan said trying to be optimistic.

"I certainly hope it doesn't. You could lose everything, sweetheart. Not to mention my reputation is on the line too, you know?"

"Yes, mom, I know. It'll be alright," she told her mother, unsure if she believed it herself. "Listen, I gotta get back to work, okay? I love you."

"I love you too, Megan. Please keep in mind that we don't hit or assault people, you understand? That's not how we settle things. I never thought I'd have to remind you of this at 30 years old."

Megan exhaled deeply. "Mom, you don't, alright? I'm sorry. I don't know what came over me, but I promise it won't happen again."

"It better not. I'll talk to you later. If worse comes to worst, you know we have a great lawyer on speed dial."

"Thanks, mom, bye." Megan hung up the phone. *Here we go again with this lawyer guy,* she thought. The last time Keres had to use her lawyer; it was against Megan's ex-boyfriend Sean. He and Megan dated for three years until one night a heated argument caused Sean to snap, and he slapped Megan across the face. Keres was extremely irate, and Sean who ironically was studying to be a lawyer himself didn't stand a chance. Keres had her lawyer threaten to end Sean's reputation and law career before it even started.

159

Keres and her lawyer worked endlessly to undermine everything Sean tried to do to get ahead. Their constant meddling eventually forced Sean to move out of the state of California so he could salvage his reputation and finish law school in peace. Megan was upset for a while but looking back she knew that her mother was just looking out for her best interest. Sean was a delight to Megan during most of their relationship. However, toward the end, he'd become ill-tempered for reasons unknown to her. For all Megan knew, the first time Sean hit her might not have been the last if her mother hadn't stepped in. For that, Megan was grateful.

"Everything okay, Meg?" Laney seemed to come out of nowhere, interrupting Megan's thoughts.

Megan sighed. "Of course Kent told my mom about last night."

"I figured," Laney said chuckling. She paused to clear her throat. "So, you and Liam, huh?"

"Are you kidding me?" Megan said throwing up her hands. "How did you find out?"

"Your brother," Laney replied, hardly able to hide her smirk.

Megan shook her head. "That boy needs to get a job," she said half-jokingly.

"Well, look, I think it's a great idea. You guys definitely get each other. And no disrespect, but your whole logic of being Liam's friend until he got married was crazy."

Megan giggled softly. "It was kind of stupid when you think about it. I was basically putting an expiration date on our friendship."

"I get it though. Things can get a bit complicated when a guy and a girl are friends, but I think you guys made the right choice by taking it a step further.

"Thanks, Laney," Megan said. "I certainly hope so."

Chapter 20

It had been three days since the incident at Mae's Kitchen, and Liam hadn't answered a single call from Shayla. The only thing she received from him was a text letting her know that he couldn't see her anymore, with no explanation. This only made Shayla angrier and she wasn't about to let a man like Liam go that easily.

She found herself parked in front of Liam's building at half-past 10 p.m. She got out of the car, walked swiftly and entered the building.

"I'm here to see Liam Franklin," Shayla told the clerk when she arrived at the front desk.

"Your name is?" he asked her.

"Shayla Henry."

She watched impatiently as he typed a few letters on the keyboard in front of him. "Uh, I'm sorry ma'am but I can't let you up to the penthouse."

"What? Why not?" Shayla frowned.

"Your name is flagged here in the system. It says not to let you up."

"There must be some sort of mistake." Shayla slammed her purse on the desk. "Call Mr. Franklin and tell him there's been a mistake. Tell him I'm here," she demanded.

"No, ma'am. I'm sorry but there's no mistake. Flags in the system are personally requested by the residents."

"But I'm his Cook," Shayla said desperately.

"Ma'am, I'm sorry. I'm going to have to ask you to leave," the clerk said politely.

"I am not leaving until I see Liam. Do you hear me? You need to call him *right* now!" Shayla was extremely loud and now disturbing the peace.

The clerk picked up the phone and waited two seconds before someone picked up on the other end.

"Yes, we have a disturbance here at the front desk. I'm going to need security ASAP."

"You little worm!" Shayla said, taking a small flowerpot and slamming it to the floor. "You called security on me?"

The clerk ducked behind the counter as Shayla sent a few more objects flying his way. Before she knew it, security scooped her up and carried her out of the building, her arms flailing about.

"I will be back with my lawyer," she threatened after the large security guard put her down.

"Ma'am, you're trespassing and disturbing the peace," said the large man. "You are lucky we didn't call the police, now go home."

"Argh!!" Shayla was beyond frustrated. Defeated, she turned on her heels and headed toward her car. She watched furiously as the security guard went back inside the building, once he saw that she was in her car.

As she pulled off, she dialed Liam's number, but he didn't answer. Her blood boiled as she drove and soon enough her face was wet from tears, and she cried all the way home.

She pulled her car into the driveway of her townhouse where she normally parked. Only, the driveway was in the back of the house, and at this time of night, the area was not well lit.

Shayla sighed deeply. A few more tears streamed down her face. She quickly wiped them away so she could search for her house keys. She found them, then grabbed her purse, stepped out of her car and locked the doors. Unfortunately for Shayla, she did not see the man in all black lurking in the darkness. As she took a few steps toward the back door of her house, she suddenly felt a gloved hand cover her mouth and yolk

164

her body a few inches from the ground. Her shoes scraped the ground here and there as she felt her body being carried off to what seemed only a few feet. Shayla's muffled screams were to no avail as there was no one around to hear them. She kicked and tried biting the man's fingers, but he only tightened his grip and pressed his gloved hand harder against her mouth. She tried stomping the heel of her stiletto into his boot, but the masked man grew tired of her struggle and violently snapped her neck. Shayla's lifeless body dropped to the ground and the man fled the scene.

Chapter 21

The news of Shayla's murder sent shock waves through the city and citizens were frantic with fear. Since the local police department hadn't dealt with murder in over twenty years, they weren't exactly sure how to handle it. So, the police chief issued a 9 p.m. curfew until further notice. Initially, the curfew was only for the citizens of Encantador Valley where Shayla lived; but then the mayor broadened the curfew to the surrounding communities within a 10-mile radius. This included the town of Golden Savannas where Megan lived and Cactus High Hill where Liam lived.

Megan heard the news of Shayla's murder this morning on the radio during her drive to work. At the time she couldn't believe what she was hearing, and her stomach was immediately in knots. Sure, she didn't like Shayla, but she most certainly didn't wish death on the girl. In Megan's opinion, no one deserved that, except the men who took her father.

Megan sat quietly at her desk with her head buried in her hands. Her stress levels were high, and the office was awfully quiet. Even with her door closed, she could hear the tip-tapping of her employees' keyboards and the dings of their email notifications in the distance.

Even Laney who was normally the busy bee of the office, was oddly quiet today. She'd come into Megan's office once just to confirm that she heard the news, and Megan didn't hear a word from her since. Yet, Megan understood that people were scared. A murder in these parts was way out of the norm for them. A burglary was even a bit farfetched, but the citizens would've accepted that far better.

Because of this, Megan had to be sympathetic to her employees. Besides, she didn't have the strength to make her rounds to ensure that everyone was working as they should've been. Instead, she came up with the idea to send out a mass email to all her employees informing them that Stone Art Enterprises was closing early today and will be closed tomorrow as well. After she sent the email, she logged off her computer and went to find Laney.

"Hey, can you lock up for me? I'm heading out now," Megan told her.

167

"Sure," Laney said. Her voice sounded a bit hoarse, and she looked weary.

"You should get going too, Laney," Megan said concerned.

"I will." Laney didn't even bother to look up from her computer screen.

Megan felt bad that she didn't know what to say to cheer Laney up. So, instead, she proceeded with her directives. "Okay, I'll see you later then. Please have everyone gone within the hour. I want fresh energy when we come back to work in two days."

"Sure," was all Laney managed to say.

◼◻◼◻◼◻◼◻◼

Megan sat anxiously at a quiet booth inside of Helena's restaurant. She asked Liam to meet her there for lunch and he was already ten minutes behind.

"Come on, Liam," she said aloud. "Where are you?" Her mind was all over the place and she hadn't heard anything from him since hearing the news this morning.

She looked up and saw Liam walking toward her, so she stood up to greet him. Liam didn't say a word, so neither did Megan. Instead, they held each other tight. Liam caressed Megan's soft curly hair, which hung past her shoulders when she didn't have it straightened. He then kissed her gently on the lips. His kiss made Megan feel like she was in heaven, and for a split second, she forgot about Shayla.

They slid into the booth on opposite sides and began browsing through the menu.

"I'm surprised you're late," Megan said sweetly.

"I apologize. I got a little tied up with my last patient."

Megan only smiled.

"So, your mother's favorite restaurant, huh?" Liam said, attempting to relieve the awkward tension. "We've never been here before. I can see why she likes it. Very fancy."

"Why haven't I heard from you all morning?" Megan asked, ignoring Liam's small talk.

Just like that, Liam's demeanor changed. He looked stressed and as far as Megan could tell, even a little worried.

"I just had to deal with a lot today." He exhaled deeply.

Megan hated to see Liam like this. It was so rare, and it made her feel helpless.

"Is everything okay?" She reached across the table and gently held Liam's hand. He looked into Megan's eyes and knew it was time to tell her what was on his mind.

"A detective came to my office this morning to question me about Shayla," Liam said ashamed.

"What?... But why?" Megan frowned.

"Because my number was the last number she dialed. She was killed about twenty minutes afterward."

"So, did you speak to her?"

"No. I haven't spoken to her since that night at Mae's Kitchen. I even texted her to tell her it was over, but she just wouldn't listen."

"Oh, No. So, are you some sort of suspect or something?" Megan was starting to feel concerned.

"I don't know, but I called my lawyer right away. He told me not to answer any questions until he arrived, so I didn't."

"You don't think that made you look even more suspicious?" Megan's paranoia was starting to set in.

"Even more suspicious?" Liam looked at Megan disbelievingly. "What are you saying, Meg?"

She didn't answer him. Instead, she thought back to the night Liam officially declared his love for her. She recalled him telling her that he knew how to handle Shayla. *"Anything for you, Meg,"* is what she remembered him saying.

"So, you're just gonna ignore me now. That's nice." Liam was frustrated and Megan was not being as supportive as he'd hoped.

"I'm sorry, Liam, but I don't know what to think about all this."

"Think about what? Don't tell me you think I'm capable of something like this."

"I didn't before, but now that the police are questioning you, I-

"You've got to be kidding me!" Liam shouted. He looked at Megan as if he didn't know who she was anymore.

"Liam?" Megan said, looking around the restaurant. "Why are you so loud?"

"Ah, who cares?" he said, fanning her off. Liam couldn't care less about Megan's embarrassment, and he was certainly done listening to her nonsense.

Megan was shocked by Liam's behavior and it made her very uncomfortable. All she could think about was her ex-boyfriend Sean violently snapping at her.

"Liam, I-I think I need to go," she said hesitantly.

"You do that then, alright? But let me say this, I wouldn't dare sacrifice myself, my freedom, and my hard-earned career for anybody. Not even you, Meg. And the fact that you believe I'm capable of something like this tells me you're not the woman I thought you were."

Megan swallowed hard. "I just need a little time, Liam. You're not yourself right now."

"I *am* myself. I'm just human and I get angry sometimes too. What?... You think you're the only one who gets to be sad and upset?"

Megan lowered her head. She couldn't answer him or look him in the eyes. If he was innocent, he had the right to lash out at her, but it was more than she could handle right now. She slowly grabbed her pocketbook and got up from the table.

"Yeah, just what I thought," Liam spat. "Maybe we should've just stayed friends, or maybe we shouldn't be that either."

Shattered, Megan burst into tears and ran out of the restaurant.

Chapter 22

After the failed lunch with Liam, Megan spent the rest of her day sulking at home. As she sat on her sofa, she couldn't believe how things were turning out. She didn't even get to enjoy one full day with Liam as her boyfriend. It was as if Shayla was still able to come between them, even in her death. Yet, the thing that troubled Megan the most was that Shayla promised to press charges on her. *What if Shayla told her lawyer about the incident before she was killed?* she thought. *Then the police will come to question me too.* The thought was too much for Megan and she needed a distraction.

She stretched her arm toward the coffee table to grab her pocketbook. Rummaging through it, she found the card to the Private Investigator. She dialed the number and waited for him to answer.

"Hello?" said a male voice on the other end.

"Hi, uh, Mr. Tassio?"

"Yes, that's me. How may I help you?" he asked politely.

"This is Megan Stone. I booked an appointment with you last week."

"Yes, yes. How are you?"

"I'm doing okay," Megan said half-heartedly. "Listen, I wanted to see if we could meet sooner."

"Sure. How soon?"

"Like, ASAP. Except, I was thinking more along the lines of me giving you some information over the phone. Can you start the investigation like that?" Megan had her fingers crossed.

"Uh, sure. That shouldn't be a problem. Let me get a pen and some paper."

Megan let out a sigh of relief. She was in no mood to meet with anybody right now. Yet, she wanted to get the ball rolling with the investigation while she looked into something else: the keys to the mausoleum.

After giving Mr. Tassio her father's and mother's full names, and other pertinent information, she hung up the phone and headed to her master bathroom. She turned on the faucets to her jacuzzi bathtub and added some lavender-scented bubble bath as the tub filled with water. She lit a few candles, let the water cool a bit, dimmed the lights, undressed, and got in. She needed this time to relax her mind, and the water felt great. She was tired of being in a state of melancholy. Her dream was to get off this emotional rollercoaster she knew as her life. However, she didn't think she had a chance at peace without first getting closure. For this reason, she planned on paying a visit to Mountain Valley Cemetery first thing in the morning.

Chapter 23

Megan parked her car along the dirt road of Mountain Valley Cemetery, just as she planned. She got out of the car and searched for her grandmother's crypt. When she finally found it, it practically fit the description of the mausoleum in Liam's story. The crypt was the size of a small chapel.

Megan used the key she copied to open the door. Since there was only one lock, she still didn't know what the second key was for. As she stepped into the crypt, she was fascinated by how splendid it was inside. There was no doubt that her mother had decked the place out. It was cooled by air conditioning, complemented with fresh beautiful flowers all over the room, and fancy looking whitewashed vintage pews. Moreover, the granite floor was top-notch, and the lighting from the crystal chandeliers gave the room a serene feel. Megan could see her grandmother's mausoleum centered at the far end of the room. It was raised slightly above the ground and there were unlit candles all around it. Megan walked down the small aisle and knelt at what looked like an altar, to pay her respects.

Nevertheless, she didn't have time to waste. She looked around the room searching for something out of the ordinary. It wasn't long before she found a medium-sized trunk against the wall behind the mausoleum. She examined the trunk and realized that it was locked. *The second key,* she thought. Megan quickly removed the set of keys from her back pocket and inserted the second one into the lock. The trunk slowly popped open.

Megan exhaled deeply. She nervously went through the items inside the trunk, which didn't seem like much. So far, all Megan could see were old pictures, trinkets, and mementos. Megan figured they belonged to her grandmother. She was about to close the trunk when she spotted a picture of her father holding a baby. She picked up the picture and smiled. She could tell that the baby was her. She wanted to take the picture with her but reminded herself that no one was supposed to know she was there. She placed the picture over her heart before putting it back where she found it. She attempted to close the trunk again but spotted a videocassette tape sticking out of the clutter of items.

"A good 'ole VHS-C, huh?" Megan said aloud. She wondered what was on the tape, only she had no way of knowing since she hadn't owned a VCR in years. Having little time to think, Megan decided to do the same thing she did when she found the keys to the crypt; make a copy and return it immediately.

She rushed out of the crypt and did a quick internet search of a local place that would copy the tape. As soon as she found one, she put the address in her GPS and drove as fast as she could.

Thankfully, the establishment that copied the tape was a vintage shop, and business was slow. Megan not only was served right away, but she was also able to buy a used VCR. The quick service allowed her to make it back to the cemetery within an hour.

Megan hastily went into the crypt, unlocked the trunk and placed the tape back where she found it. She locked the trunk, and rushed out of the crypt, locking the door behind her.

On the way home a terrible feeling of dread came over her. She had no idea where the feeling was coming from, but she wanted to shake it as soon as possible.

❏❏❏❏❏❏❏❏❏

When Megan arrived home, she couldn't wait to watch the tape. She fed Cooper who hounded her as soon as she got into the house, then she ran upstairs to her bedroom and closed the door. She turned on the TV and hooked up the VCR. She placed the tape into the adapter, then took a deep breath before inserting it into the VCR. "Here we go," she said and pressed play.

Immediately, Megan could see her father on the screen. He was laughing and smiling as he talked to the man behind the camera. It took a little while for Megan to realize that the camera man's voice belonged to Uncle Stan. For a little while, Megan enjoyed watching her father interact with the camera. He seemed so full of life, and it made her smile. Then just like that, she missed him even more.

Just then, Megan's cell phone rang. She paused the video and answered almost impatiently.

"Hello," she said dryly.

"Hi, Megan, It's Jim Tassio. I don't have a lot of time, but I just wanted to let you know that I found some information."

Wow, that was fast, Megan thought, but then said; "what did you find?"

"Your mother has a connection with someone named Dave Gallows. I'm not sure what kind of connection but I know it might be a pretty strong one since they've had dealings for over twenty years."

"Are you sure?" Megan couldn't believe it.

"Yes. Now is there anything you'd like to add before I continue with the investigation?"

"Uh-uh, there is one thing," Megan hesitated. "I've been a little suspicious lately about my brother's paternity. Do you think you could check that out as far as Dave goes?"

"I could check it out, but so far there's nothing that suggests that Dave and your mother were ever romantically involved. But like I said, I'll check it out."

"Thanks," Megan said, then ended the call. She wanted to rip her hair out. Her mother was somehow associated with Dave Gallows and she didn't even know it. For the most part, it wasn't a surprise since her mother practically knew everyone. Yet, knowing Dave for over twenty years made Megan wonder. She didn't know how she immediately went into suspecting Dave of being Kent's father, but she wanted to cover all angles, so she went for it.

What am I getting myself into? she thought. It was a question she found herself asking more than she wanted. *Whatever happens, I just hope Kent doesn't get mad at me.*

Chapter 24

After Megan ended her call with Mr. Tassio, she went back to watching the home-made video. As Megan looked on, her father shared a few words, which were almost speech-like. He kept referring to Stan as "your Uncle Stan" and kept saying words like "your mother and me." Before long, Megan figured it out. The video was addressed to her.

She watched on and moments later her mother came waddling over to her father who helped her sit on a couch. Then another woman appeared. She was very pretty and of a yellow boned complexion like Keres, only they looked nothing alike. The woman had brown eyes and a narrow face with soft features, a small shapely frame, and her hair loosely pinned up. Her father walked over to the woman, and what happened next threw Megan for a loop. "Sweetheart, it took you long enough," her father said, then he kissed the other woman on the lips right in front of her mother. Megan was surprised when Keres didn't react. She intensely watched on with furrowed brows and confusion as her father led the other woman to the couch as well. The three sat together with Megha in the middle. Then the other woman spoke. "Hi sweetie, I know you're not here with us yet, but we can't wait to meet you," she said as she rubbed Keres' pregnant belly.

"Why isn't my mother saying anything?" Megan said under her breath. The video was starting to creep her out. Then her father spoke again. "That's right, baby. We are so excited for your arrival. We never thought this would've been possible, but Keres here stepped in and did us the honor of being our surrogate mom."

Megan couldn't believe what she just heard. She suddenly seemed to be having an out of body experience, although she wasn't. Still, her head was spinning, and she felt as if she was floating in mid-air. She thought she was hallucinating as she heard her father's voice carry on. Only it seemed to be in the distance; ringing and echoing in her head. Then she heard the woman's voice echo, "Mommy loves you, honey, and if I could've carried you myself I would've. But you have my DNA and that's all that matters."

Megan let out a blood-curdling scream. "Nooooooo," she cried hysterically. "This can't be right." She continued to cry and scream until everything unexpectedly went black.

❑❑❑❑❑❑❑❑❑

When Megan finally gained consciousness, she heard Cooper's paws scratching at her bedroom door. He'd come once he heard her scream, but Megan was passed out for quite a while, so Cooper stayed by her door scratching and crying the whole time.

Megan's head was still spinning, and Cooper's whimpering didn't help.

"It's okay, Coop," Megan yelled out, wanting him to shut up. She felt as though she could hardly move, so she lay sprawled out on the carpet a bit longer. Her mind raced as fast as lightning could travel and she could hardly process one thought before a new one came. She didn't even know how to begin to process what she discovered in the video. Keres not being her mother didn't make sense to her and it didn't feel right. Or maybe it didn't feel right because she didn't want it to. All Megan knew was that she lived a lie her whole life. Keres was not her mother, which made Kent her half-brother. To add insult to injury, her father, who had never given her a reason to doubt him, had played a part in the lie as well, and so did

Uncle Stan. It all hurt too much to think about, and all she could do was cry even more.

Chapter 25

A week had gone by since Megan discovered the heartbreaking revelation of her parentage and she practically withdrew herself from everyone she knew. Since watching the video, she went to work once and ignored everyone throughout the entire day. Before leaving, she told Laney to serve as second in command since she would be out of the office for a while. It raised a red flag for Laney, so she alerted Kent and Liam that something was off with Megan. Liam tried reaching out to Megan once via text, but she didn't respond. However, Kent was relentless. It got so bad that he went to Megan's house and caused a scene in her front yard; shouting her name, then banging on her front door, injured leg and all. Eventually, he threatened to call the police to come and break down the door if she didn't let him in. After all that, Megan finally gave in, but when she opened the door, she politely asked Kent to leave. When he refused, she promised him that she would answer his texts from then on and let him know that she just needed some time to herself. Kent wasn't fully on board, but he could see that Megan didn't look herself. She appeared drained and her eyes were puffy and red. So, he unwillingly decided to respect her wishes and leave. Since that day, Megan kept her promise and responded whenever Kent texted to check on her.

Keres also tried to call Megan a few times after Kent told her something was wrong. But Megan gave her the same treatment. The calls from Keres stopped once Kent told her to give Megan some space.

Megan was officially in a dark place in her life. Her state of mind was causing her to make decisions that weren't very conducive to her mental health. She hardly ate or showered, and her appearance had become disheveled. On top of that, she stopped seeing Dr. Green.

For the most part, Megan locked herself in her room, so even Cooper could stay away. But, today was different from the rest. Today Megan decided to leave her house and go for a drive. She climbed out of bed, brushed her teeth, washed her face, threw on some sweatpants and a t-shirt, barely brushed her hair into a ponytail, and left the house.

She jumped into her car, sped down the driveway and down the road. Megan had no clue where she was going, and she didn't care. The fresh air was long overdue, and she had a good mind to drive to another state or across the border. At this point, Megan felt alone in the world. Although she had people who loved her and were concerned about her, she didn't see it that way. For everyone she knew in her life, there was a reason why she couldn't confide in them. She couldn't talk to Kent about Keres not being her real mother because he'd just run and tell mommy as he had always done. She couldn't talk to Laney about it because she never let Laney that deep into her personal life. She couldn't talk to Liam because of the whole Shayla ordeal, and he creeped her out the last time they spoke. Lastly, Megan couldn't talk to Dr. Green because she was in no mood to dive deep into her feelings. Besides, when it came to discussing Liam, Megan was afraid she might give Dr. Green incriminating evidence against him; even though their sessions were strictly confidential. For these reasons, Megan's car ride to nowhere would just have to do.

Megan drove aimlessly for an hour straight. She finally came to a quiet town where the streets were narrow, and she saw at least one to two people here and there. *What is this place?* she thought. As she drove further down the narrow road, she saw a big sign in front of a church that read: CAST ALL YOUR CARES ON GOD, FOR HE CARES FOR YOU! Megan found the sign interesting. She never thought of God caring about her or her problems. She kept driving down the road but suddenly had a strange feeling that she should turn around. She hesitated for a moment, then made a U-turn. As Megan drove back down the road, she felt a nudging to turn into the church parking lot. She pulled into the small lot, parked her car, and went inside.

Megan had no clue what she was doing inside the church, but she felt it in her heart to be there. Truthfully, she was never aware that churches opened on weekdays, and this was a strange way to find out. As Megan walked down the aisle of the small church, she stopped midway and took a seat. She was unsure of what to do, so she sat in silence. The atmosphere had a peaceful feel to it, but then again, she was the only one there, or so she thought.

"God bless you, sister," said a kind but deep voice.

Megan turned around to see who the voice belonged to.

"Hello," she said to an elderly Latino man with a head full of white hair.

"I'm Pastor Tomas Valdez, but you can call me Pastor Tom." His eyes were trusting, and his smile warmed the heart.

"Nice to meet you, Pastor Tom." Megan stood up to shake his hand. "I'm Megan."

"Please, please, sit down, Megan." He gestured for her to retake her seat and sat down in the chair behind her. "Don't mind me, but what brings you in? We rarely get visitors, since all of our attendees are members."

"Believe it or not, I was just going for a drive and when I saw the sign, I felt drawn to it. Does that sound weird?" Megan hoped she didn't sound like a lunatic.

"Not at all. It sounds like God."

Megan didn't know how to receive his response, but there was something about his pleasant aura that put her at ease.

"I'm afraid I don't know much about God. I believe in Him, but I don't know Him?" she confessed.

"Well, I think He wants to know you, even though He already does," Pastor Tom smiled gently.

"If He already knows me, why would He *want* to know me?" Megan was confused.

"Well, what God really wants is a relationship with you. For instance, He knows about all your problems, but if you look elsewhere for help with those problems instead of looking to God, He'll most likely allow you to figure it out on your own."

"But what if I can't figure it out, or don't figure it out?" she said hopelessly.

"Oh, you can't, and you won't," Pastor Tom informed her. "You see, the Bible teaches us that there is a way that seems right to a man, but in the end, it leads to death. This is found in Proverbs 14:12. So, if you go through life thinking you know it all, you make no room for God in your heart. On top of that, your path will eventually lead to destruction. But the good news is, He'll step in, only if you let Him."

"How do I let Him?"

"You only need to ask, then let go of the reins."

"Let go of the reins?" Megan repeated, confused.

"Let God be in control," he answered kindly.

Megan nodded. Letting God be in control of her life was foreign to her, but at this point, she was desperate for peace and out of options.

Megan talked with Pastor Tom for a total of three hours. Not once did she have to tell him about her life's issues and all the things she was going

190

through. Still, somehow talking to Pastor Tom was therapeutic and enlightening. He was full of wisdom and his kindness was magnetic. Megan was thankful that she listened to her heart and made that U-turn.

Before Megan left, Pastor Tom prayed for her, then asked her if she wanted to accept Jesus as her Lord and Savior. He let her know that no one could get to the Father without going through the Son. Megan happily agreed, then Pastor Tom led her in a prayer to accept Christ. He also gave her an informational pamphlet and a Bible to take home with her. Megan had no idea that she would leave her house today and return home a saved woman. *It was all God,* she thought, smiling.

Chapter 26

Megan knew that her problems were far from over, but after her time with Pastor Tom, she regained her strength. The next day she went back to work and it was business as usual. Laney was relieved to have her back, to say the least.

As Megan sat at her desk, her cell phone rang and Mr. Tassio's name came up on the caller ID.

"Got anything new?" Megan said cutting right to the chase.

"As a matter of fact, I do. I found out that Dave Gallows is involved in some criminal activity. I'm not sure what it is yet, but I believe it has something to do with smuggling, and he's using Gashange's gallery to do it."

"Oh, my goodness," Megan whispered into the phone.

"There's something else."

Megan could hear the seriousness of Mr. Tassio's tone. "What is it?" she said dreadfully.

"Your father knew Dave Gallows as well. I believe he may have gotten himself involved with some of the illegal activities at Gashange's."

"Anything else?" she said dryly.

"Uh, yeah. Your mother might be related to Dave."

Megan raised a brow. "What?... Related how?"

"I'm not sure, but I'm working on that. I suspect that she might be the reason why your father got involved with Dave in the first place."

Megan sighed. "Well, thank you for the update."

"Sure thing," Mr. Tassio replied, then hung up.

Megan wasn't surprised at all that her father might've been involved in criminal activity. It was something her mother already told her. However, she was surprised to hear that her father also knew Dave and that her mother might've been the reason her father got caught up.

Still, after everything she had learned, the one chapter she could close for sure was that Dave was not Kent's father, and neither was Uncle Stan. After having nothing but time to think, she'd come to realize that it was *her* parentage in question all along, not Kent's. All the digging and snooping she did on her brother's behalf, only to find that Megha was indeed his father, but Keres was not her mother. After gathering up enough courage, Megan went back to watch the video in its entirety the night before she went back to work. It was then that she learned her real mother's name; Joanna. Megan even realized that she looked more like her birth mother than she did her father; only with darker skin. To Megan, Joanna seemed to be a loving and kind person. She now wanted to know what happened to her. Megan decided to finally confront the only person who could provide her with answers; Keres.

□◦□◦□◦□◦□

The next day, Megan sat on her couch trying to figure out how she would confront her mother. However, before she left the office yesterday, she called Mr. Tassio back and asked him to stake out her mother's house. Megan wanted him to keep tabs on Keres so that she knew when she was coming or going. She didn't want to go over there and find that her mother wasn't home. Megan also knew that calling wouldn't help since Keres didn't do well with answering her calls.

So far, Mr. Tassio reported that Keres was gone all evening yesterday and a good portion of the afternoon. He also told Megan that she left out around 4:30 p.m. and hasn't returned. It was now 6:00 p.m. and Megan wished her mother would return soon because her nerves were starting to get the best of her.

Just then she received a text from Mr. Tassio telling her that Keres just arrived home. Megan let him know that she was on her way. She did some breathing exercises, said a quick prayer, then dashed out the door.

When she arrived at her mother's house, she used her key to let herself in. "Mom?" she called. "Mom, where are you?"

"In here, sweetheart," her mother called from the kitchen.

Megan rushed into the kitchen where she found her mother slicing an apple over a medium-sized bowl. Megan figured Keres was preparing a fruit salad after spotting other fruit in the bowl.

"What are you doing here, Meg?" Keres asked surprised. "I thought you were taking time for yourself?"

"I was, but I had to get back to work."

"Well, I'm glad you finally decided to show your face." Keres flashed her a smile.

Megan only returned a half-smile. "Mom, can I talk to you? Maybe out on the back porch where we can have some privacy?"

"Megan, this better not be any more mess about your father," Keres warned. "I told you, I'm over it and I am not going to entertain it."

"It's not. I promise," Megan replied.

"Alright then, you go on ahead. Let me just get a lid for this fruit and I'll be right there."

Megan proceeded to the back porch which was enclosed with glass. She sat on a comfortable outdoor loveseat and waited for her mother to join her.

Keres came out shortly after and sat in a cushioned wicker chair across from Megan.

"What's going on?" Keres asked, uninterestingly.

Megan cleared her throat. *Here goes,* she thought. "Mom, I've been snooping around lately, and-

"Snooping around where?" Keres interrupted sharply.

Megan exhaled deeply. "In your room, and at grandma's mausoleum." Megan nervously watched as a look of sheer terror came across her mother's face.

"H-how did you get into my mother's mausoleum?" Keres was stunned and thought she might lose it.

"I- I found a set of keys in your desk, and I made copies."

"Why would you do that?! Why?" Keres burned with anger.

"I needed answers, that's why!" Megan shouted back. "This is all your fault. If only you had told me everything I needed to know, I would've never felt the need to go behind your back."

Keres' face was almost beet red and her breathing became viciously rapid. Megan felt as though she was watching a scene from a horror movie, and that Keres would turn into a werewolf at any moment.

"You have gone too far," Keres seethed.

Unfazed by Keres' fury, Megan boldly spoke. "No, I think you're the one who's gone too far, *mom*. Or should I call you *Keres* the *surrogate?*" Megan's last statement had the women now involved in a tensed staring match; Keres with her evil glare, and Megan with her intrepid gaze. Only, Keres' icy blue eyes were more piercing and caused Megan to eventually look away.

Suddenly, Keres' demeanor changed drastically, and she became very calm. Megan wasn't sure what to make of it, but she didn't trust it. She never saw her mother in this light before, and it was awfully strange.

"So, what now?" Keres half-whispered.

Megan shrugged. "I wanna know what happened to Joanna, my real mother."

"She died," Keres said with no feeling.

"How?" Megan asked mildly.

"In a car accident." Keres sat back and folded her arms.

"Well, why did my dad marry you if you were just a surrogate?"

"Because your father didn't want you growing up without a mother. And what better choice than the woman already carrying you?"

Megan nodded sadly. She didn't know much, but that sounded like something her father would do.

"Is there anything else?" Keres asked in a cool but creepy voice.

"Yes. Dave Gallows, who is he?"

The question infuriated Keres but she tried her hardest to remain calm. "He's my uncle," she said through gritted teeth. "How did you find out about him?"

"Why didn't you ever tell us about him? Megan asked, ignoring Keres' question.

Keres exhaled sharply. "If you must know, my father was Dave's older brother. My father had an affair with my mother and abandoned her once she got pregnant with me. He wanted nothing to do with the shame associated with being with a black woman or having a black child."

"Was he racist or something?" Megan asked curiously.

"No, but many of his colleagues were, and so was his wife," Keres said, annoyed. She was in no mood for interrogation but continued, seeing that Megan would be relentless if she hadn't. "I guess guilt must've eaten away at my father over the years. After a while, he had Dave check on my mother and me every so often to make sure we had everything we needed. But I never met him. I just know he had blue eyes, like mine. Anyway, we were sworn to secrecy if we wanted to continue getting the help. And that's how it's always been, even after my so-called father was dead and gone." Keres looked away, still visibly irritated. She took a moment to gain her composure, then directed her attention back to Megan. "Now, how did you find out about Dave?" she said, scowling.

"I hired a PI. He's been helping me tie up some very loose ends," Megan said as she tried to hide her uneasiness.

"Megan, sweetheart, you should've stopped at Joanna," Keres' tone was threatening. "Digging into Dave Gallows is a mistake."

"Why?... Am I gonna vanish like my father did?" Megan was the one angry now.

"If you don't stop your PI from investigating Dave, I can't promise your safety," Keres said seriously. "I told you this whole PI thing was a bad idea anyway, but you just couldn't listen."

Megan was completely shaken. Even after everything she'd heard, she couldn't believe that Keres would let Dave hurt her. Tears streamed down her face.

"Is it that easy for you?" she sobbed. "You wouldn't let him hurt Kent, right? But me...I'm nothing."

"That is not true, and you know it."

"I don't know anything anymore," Megan cried uncontrollably. "You probably never even loved me."

Seeing Megan cry made Keres uncomfortable, but she didn't have it in her heart to console her. Instead, she decided to prove Megan wrong.

"You think I never loved you?" Keres asked. "I've always loved you and have always protected you. I carried you for nine months, surrogate or not, you are my daughter!" Keres was now shouting again. Only this time she didn't look so angry. "And you wanna know what else?" she said continuing.

Megan wiped her tears with her t-shirt. "What?" she whispered.

Keres glared at Megan menacingly and said: "I did anything for you."

A sudden chill went up Megan's spine. "What do you mean, *anything?*"

"I *mean,* my love for you went beyond measure, and I never let anyone hurt you without paying the cost." Keres now had a deranged expression on her face.

Megan sat speechless while Keres carried on. "Remember that boyfriend of yours, Sean? I took care of him for you, didn't I?"

"Yes, and I'm grateful for that, but sending him away wasn't your choice to make. He just up and left, and I never got any closure from that," Megan sniffled.

"He didn't just up and leave. I killed him, honey." Keres let out a sinister laugh. "He had to go. If he did it once, he would've done it again."

Megan was horrified at her mother's confession. *There's no way I'm hearing this,* she thought, *no way.* Megan immediately began to scan her brain of any memory that would prove true to what her mother was saying. She thought back to the day when Sean's sister came asking her about his whereabouts. Oddly enough, it was no cause for alarm to Megan. As far as she was concerned, Sean had changed so drastically, and she'd become accustomed to him doing things out of character, including disappearing for days on end. But there was no way she was going to tell Sean's sister that her mother ran him out of town. The only answer Megan had for his sister was that they had broken up and she hadn't heard from him in weeks. That was the truth, and after that, Megan never heard from Sean's sister again.

"You didn't, please tell me you didn't," Megan said desperately.

"Well, *I* didn't, but somebody did, and I paid good money for it," Keres smirked. "Just like I paid for your little Sheila problem to go away."

Megan frowned. "Y--You mean *Shayla?*"

"That's the one," Keres said casually. "You don't think I was gonna let her press charges on you, do you? She would've ruined everything you worked so hard for."

"No, you couldn't have," Megan said, shaking her head in disbelief. "You said it yourself, we don't settle things with violence."

"No, I said we don't *hit* people," Keres corrected. "I never said anything against putting a hit on a person." Keres cracked up as if she'd just told the funniest joke ever.

"I can't - I- I don't believe this," Megan said, tears streaming down her face again.

"You *can't* or you *don't?*" Keres asked mockingly. "Because I've got more. You wanted it, now I'm gonna give it to you, once and for all so you can finally SHUT UP!" Keres' voice was loud but unexpectedly deeper. Almost as if she was possessed by a demon.

Megan sat still as if spellbound, with nothing to do but listen. All the while the tears never stopped streaming.

"Hmph. What the heck, let the tears flow," Keres taunted. "Your real mother, Joanna, was weak too. Sweet, but weak. How would she have handled Sean, huh?" Keres slowly walked over to Megan, sat beside her, and stroked her hair. "Of course, we'll never know now, because I took care of that problem too. She was an obstacle for me. As long as she was around, I couldn't have the man I wanted...or the baby I wanted. So, I made sure to slip a little mickey in her morning coffee before she left for work." Keres flashed an evil grin.

Megan finally looked up at Keres, but still couldn't say anything.

"That's right," Keres said, moving on with her story. "It worked quicker than I expected, too. She fell asleep behind the wheel just halfway down the road and crashed into a tree. Your father was devastated, but he got over it, and we moved on together." Keres paused thoughtfully. "Of course, he had to go messing things up when his curiosity got the best of him. I guess that's where you get it from, huh? Anyway, once the word got out that Megha was asking questions, not even I could save him from the wrath of my Uncle Dave."

Megan finally broke her silence. "I'd like to go now, please."

"Oh, isn't that interesting? You wanted the answers, now you got them, and you don't like them," Keres teased.

Megan instantly recalled Liam telling her the same thing a couple of weeks ago when she asked him about the keys to the mausoleum.

"Go ahead then," Keres told her. Megan slowly got up and began walking toward the porch exit.

"Megan," Keres called before she could fully exit the porch.

"Yes," Megan responded faintly.

"If you say a word about this to anyone, I will send the police to your gallery and have you arrested for smuggling weapons."

"Smuggling weapons?" Megan said, perplexed. She was too drained for any more of the back and forth with Keres, but now her livelihood was on the line. "I'm not smuggling any weapons," she retorted. Now she knew how Liam felt for being falsely accused.

"Oh, but you are now. You see, the moment your stupid little assistant made a deal with Dave, she made a deal with the devil. Now, make sure you don't say anything, or prison will be your new home. Either that or I could just have one of the bombs detonated in your gallery; killing your employees... your choice," Keres said coldly.

Bewildered and exhausted, Megan said; "fine, I won't say anything." Then defeatedly, she left her mother's house.

On the drive home, Megan felt completely numb. It was a miracle that she was even driving since she didn't seem coherent. In less than a month she had discovered that the woman she knew as her mother was not only *not* her biological mother but also a cold and twisted, homicidal maniac.

◘◘◘◘◘◘◘◘◘

The next day, Keres was arrested and charged with murder in the first degree, murder for hire, and conspiracy to commit murder. Dave Gallows and Sam

Shang were also arrested and charged with money laundering, drug trafficking and smuggling weapons of mass destruction. It turned out that Sam Shang was the criminal mastermind behind importing small but vastly destructive explosives from China. The weapons were hidden in the back of art paintings and imbedded in sculptures. It was the largest drug bust and terrorist infiltration in the history of San Diego. Dave Gallows was also charged with the abduction and disappearance of Megha Stone. However, he could not be charged with murder since there were no remains found and no confession on his part.

Moreover, Keres' little warning speech to Megan about not snitching, went through one ear and out the other. Only, Megan didn't have to say anything. All she had to do was let the recording speak for itself.

The day before Megan went to confront her mother, not only did she have Mr. Tassio stake out the house, but while Keres was away, he installed a recording system into the walls of her back porch. This was the same built-in recording system Megan learned about during her first session with Dr. Green.

While asking her mother to sit and talk with her on the back porch was all a part of Megan's plan, she never expected the current turn of events. Megan only wanted to record the conversation in case Keres said something incriminating against Dave Gallows. Before all this, Megan thought her mother's biggest crime was lying about being her birth mother.

When it was all said and done, Megan wanted the police to keep her name out of everything. She didn't want the extra attention and she didn't want to be a target for anybody still affiliated with Dave Gallows or Sam Shang.

Chapter 27

The past few days were a whirlwind of emotions for Megan. She didn't know whether she was coming or going. To make things worse, Kent had sunk into a deep depression and was hardly speaking to her. However, Megan knew he wasn't upset with her. He just needed time to process everything, just as she had when her world came crashing down around her.

Her questions had all been answered, except the question of her father's remains. But she decided not to dwell on it for now and move on. It was time to finally work toward her happiness. This meant living in peace, strengthening her relationship with God, and reconciliation.

Megan stepped off the elevator and knocked on the only door on the floor. The door opened and a wave of emotions crashed over her as Liam stood before her. She said nothing at all, but stared at him for a moment, then burst into tears and fell into his arms.

"Whoa, whoa. It's okay," Liam said as he held her tight. He gently guided her past the threshold and closed the door. "I gotchu. Shh, shh." He leaned his back up against the wall and slowly slid down to the floor, holding Megan the whole way down.

"I'm so sorry, Liam," Megan sobbed into his chest. "I should've believed you."

"Shh, it's okay, Meg." He lightly caressed her hair.

"Can you ever forgive me?" she said, looking up at him with pleading eyes. "I was selfish when you needed me the most. I promise I won't ever let you down again."

"I know, sweetie," he said kindly. He kissed her forehead and wiped her tears. "I forgive you, now please forgive me for the horrible things I've said to *you.*"

"Of course," she whispered softly.

Liam slowly slipped off Megan's shoes, then stood and carefully helped her up from the floor. He took her by the hand and led her over to the sofa, then sat down and pulled her into his arms again. She curled her legs up on the sofa and nestled her head in his chest. Intoxicated by the mixture of his cologne and natural masculine scent, she pressed herself deeper into him, and there she felt at peace. Liam grabbed the remote control, kicked his legs up on the ottoman, and gently caressed Megan's soft hair. He quietly flipped through the channels, all the while continuously running his fingers over her hair until she finally fell sound asleep. It was the best sleep Megan had in a long, long time.

Epilogue

Five months later, Dave Gallows, Sam Shang, and Keres Danes were tried and convicted of their crimes. They were all to spend the rest of their lives behind bars. However, Keres was given the possibility of parole if she agreed to testify against Dave for his involvement in Megha's abduction and suspected killing. Keres agreed without hesitation, while also giving up the man she hired to kill Shayla. In turn, murder was added to the list of Dave's convicted crimes. Unfortunately for Keres, she won't be eligible for parole until after serving 25 years.

As for Megan, the recording proved that Laney knew nothing about Dave's plan to store smuggled weapons at Stone Art Enterprises, immediately clearing both their names. Fortunately, with Gashange's gallery closed, and the new ongoing contract with the Sanders Gallery, Stone Art Enterprises is more successful than ever. On top of that, Megan promoted Laney to Assistant Supervisor. She presently holds down the fort while Megan visits her grandmother in Sri Lanka, with Liam by her side.

◨◧◨◧◨◧◨◧◨

    Megan sat with her grandmother for the first time in over a decade. Her grandmother went back to Sri Lanka about five years after Megha's disappearance and the contact between her and Megan had been little to none. As they sat and talked, they also laughed and cried, and laughed some more. Megan could almost see her father's face as she looked at her grandmother's. Paama is what she called her; short for Aapaama, the name for paternal grandmothers in Sri Lanka.

    Megan sat and admired her grandmother's beautiful uncracked dark skin, her long, silver waist-length braid, and her straight nose and high cheekbones. *Just beautiful,* Megan thought proudly. Although Paama was very healthy, Megan didn't know how much time her grandmother had left on this Earth. Which is why it was important for Megan to come to Sri Lanka and spend two weeks with her.

Today marked Day 1, and Megan just wanted to soak it all in.

Liam, who had been sitting outside, taking in the Sri Lankan sun, suddenly entered the house carrying a few bags.

"Where should I put these, ma'am?" he asked Paama.

"On the table please," she replied sweetly.

"Where did you get those bags?" Megan said curiously.

"Oh, a man pulled up with them and asked me to bring them inside. He said he's coming in with the rest."

"Yes, I am going to make a special dinner just for you," said Paama, kissing Megan's hand. Her Tamil accent was strong but clear.

Megan smiled. Just then, a middle-aged man, about 6ft tall walked into the house carrying the rest of the bags just as Liam said he would. The man had a small afro of curly hair with colors of salt and pepper. The silkiness of his curls caused the gray to shine like polished silver. "You have company," he stated to Paama as he placed the bags on the table next to the others.

"Yes," was all Paama said.

The man turned around to greet Megan but stopped in his tracks when his eyes met hers. Megan wasn't sure if the man was crazy or just acting weird, but something was off.

As the man blankly stared at Megan, Paama kept quiet while Liam looked confused. Megan became very uncomfortable and decided to introduce herself to get past the awkward moment.

"Hi, I'm Meg-

Before she could finish telling the man her name, tears streamed down his face as he continued to stare at her. Megan paused to study the man closely, and just like that, her heart nearly sank to her feet.

She shook her head in disbelief, then whispered: "Daddy?"

The man nodded. "It's me, baby girl."

An intense feeling of warmth flashed over Megan's face and throughout her upper body. She suddenly felt lightheaded and began hyperventilating. Before anyone knew it, Megan passed out into her father's arms.

It didn't take Megan much time to regain consciousness, and once she did, she took a moment to examine her father's face once more. It was certainly him; still handsome, but aged. She wrapped her arms around his neck and hugged and squeezed him tight. The two cried softly as they lovingly embraced one another.

As the day went by, they had much to talk about, and of course, Megha had a lot of explaining to do. So, when it was all said and done, Megha informed his daughter that Keres convinced him to become a silent partner at Gashange's. However, when Megha became suspicious of certain business dealings, he began asking simple questions. Megha revealed that after his questions went unanswered, he moved to dissolve his partnership. Dave Gallows took it as a slight and Megha no longer felt safe. So, he turned to his brother Qurban, the identical twin that no one knew he had. No one knew about Qurban because he worked for the CIA. Once Megha confided in his brother about the suspicious behavior at Gashange's, Qurban went rogue and infiltrated their plans. He found out about the weapons, and their plot to abduct and kill Megha. Qurban, having no wife or children, wanted to protect his younger twin brother. So, he sent Megha away to Sri Lanka and took his place.

It also turned out that Uncle Stan's suspicion about the abductors taking Megha to clean out his accounts before killing him was close to accurate. The only difference was that the money was to be wired to an offshore account.

During that time, Qurban hacked into the offshore account and discovered that the recipient would be Dave Gallows. Qurban granted Megha access to that account so when the transfers were made, Megha would be the one to retrieve them instantly. For this to work successfully, Qurban instructed Megha to babysit the offshore account for days on end until the transfer was completed. It was crucial for Megha to retrieve the money before Dave did. Thankfully, the plan was a success and Dave never found out what happened with the money.

Megan was in awe of her father's story. She could hardly believe she was sitting there listening to him tell it. No matter how elated she was to be with her father again, sad things had taken place and their family had gone through a lot of turmoil. There was lots of lost time between them, but thanks to Uncle Qurban, whose act of selfless love and sacrifice made it possible for the remaining Stone family to rebuild and make up for the time lost.

Megha, on the other hand, was hardly stunned by what Megan told him about Keres. Toward the end of their time together, he knew she wasn't the good person she pretended to be. Still, he did not doubt that she would take care of his children. Yet, it didn't make leaving them any easier. However, he was saddened to hear that Keres was behind Joanna's death. If he had known, there was no way he would've married her. Joanna was the love of his life.

As for his feelings toward Uncle Stan, Megha was grateful to hear about how his friend stepped up for his family. His only wish was that he could talk to Stan and thank him in person. Unfortunately, that was out of the question. Megha now lived under a different alias and his identity was to remain a secret. It was the last promise he made to his brother, and he intended to keep it, even if it meant that his children would never see him again. As tempted as he was over the years to break that promise, his will power always reminded him that he couldn't let his twin's sacrifice go in vain. Qurban always told Megha that the family would reunite someday. Even though there was no way to be sure, Qurban just had faith that it would happen. After being reunited with his daughter, Megha could thankfully say that his brother's sacrifice finally paid off. He had Paama to thank as well; since he knew she surprised him with Megan's visit.

That night, before they gathered at the table for dinner, Megha pulled his daughter to the side.

"You know, it's okay if you miss Keres," he said sympathetically. "Joanna was your biological mother, but Keres was the mother that raised you."

Megan only nodded.

"I know she did a lot of terrible things; I do. But I also know you're hurting, baby girl."

"I do miss her," Megan said, as tears welled up.

"I know," he said hugging her. "You don't have to exclude her from your life, you know? Just don't tell her about me."

Megan gave her father a puzzled look. Then they burst with laughter.

"But seriously, take all the time you need, baby girl. But the forgiveness part needs to happen sooner than later, for your sake."

Megan smiled, then hugged her father tight. She just couldn't get over the fact that she was here, listening to him impart his wisdom again. After everything she had lost, the moment was bittersweet. Still, being with her father again gave her new hope.

"Daddy, the day they took you - - I mean your brother, he said something to me before he left."

"Oh, yeah, what was that?"

"He said 'remember to assess the situation.' I didn't know what that meant at the time, and maybe I still don't, but I never forgot it. I thought it was you, trying to tell me something."

Megha smiled sadly. "That was my brother trying to tip you off in some way. It wasn't part of the plan, but I guess he wanted to raise your suspicions."

"Well, I guess it worked, because here we are," Megan shrugged. "Thanks to him, I was suspicious of *everything*, literally.

They laughed in unison and headed to the dining room for dinner.

■◻■◻■◻■◻■

The following days were pure bliss and the Stone family along with Liam cherished each other's company. Over the course of those days, Kent was flown in under emergency pretenses and got the shock of his life when he was reunited with his father. The reunion was very emotional as Kent wept for nearly a half-hour.

Megan also started a painting of her mother, Joanna, after her father gave her an old picture of her. The piece was coming along well, and she planned on gifting it to him before she went back home. She decided to stay an extra week to give herself some time to finish it, and to spend more time with her father and Paama.

However, Liam had to stick to the original plan and get back to the U.S for work. The night before he left, Paama cooked a large dinner for the family. It was during that time that Liam asked for Megan's hand in marriage. The family watched in joyous anticipation as they waited for Megan to answer. Then she made Liam the happiest man on Earth when she said: "yes." Megha couldn't be prouder, and he approved of Liam one hundred percent.

As Megan looked around the table, she saw that her family wasn't complete. Nevertheless, she finally found peace within, and it was time to start counting her blessings. She was going to marry the love of her life and hopefully start a family one day. Her father was alive and well, and so was her Paama and Kent. Most importantly, she found her Lord and Savior Jesus Christ. Things were looking up, and she loved it.

The End

"The latter glory of this house shall be greater than the former, says the LORD of hosts. And in this place, I will give peace, declares the LORD of hosts."
Haggai 2:9 ESV

Made in the USA
Columbia, SC
20 September 2019